Secrets at Selwyn Castle

Beau Monde Secrets, Book 1

Anne Rollins

ARE YOU SIGNED UP FOR DRAGONBLADE'S BLOG?

You'll get the latest news and information on exclusive giveaways, exclusive excerpts, coming releases, sales, free books, cover reveals and more.

Check out our complete list of authors, too!

No spam, no junk. That's a promise!

Sign Up Here

www.dragonbladepublishing.com

Dearest Reader;

Thank you for your support of a small press. At Dragonblade Publishing, we strive to bring you the highest quality Historical Romance from some of the best authors in the business. Without your support, there is no 'us', so we sincerely hope you adore these stories and find some new favorite authors along the way.

Happy Reading!

CEO, Dragonblade Publishing

Chapter One

Monday, December 18, 1815

"IT'S SMALLER THAN I expected," Ivy exclaimed when she finally caught her first glimpse of the castle.

Selwyn Castle stood on a hill overlooking the river. The gravel drive leading to the castle passed over a diminutive arched stone bridge, meandered through the wooded valley surrounding the river, then climbed to the top of the hill. Because the trees obscured the road ahead, Ivy did not get a good view of the castle until her uncle's carriage reached the top of the hill.

She had imagined an enormous, imposing house, like Highclere Castle in Hampshire. Compared to Highclere, Selwyn Castle looked like a modest domicile. True, the front of the house boasted a high, square, crenellated tower, into which the front door led. Ivy guessed that the castle probably contained a Great Hall, a remnant of a distant past. The rest of the house had obviously been built later. It was compact and lower than the tower—three stories high rather than four.

"It is still much larger than Rufford Manor," her uncle pointed out. "And it is not the only estate belonging to the Earl of Inglewhite."

Lord Rufford was a baron, but he owned only one estate, and

much of his fortune was invested in trade—a thing the aristocracy frowned upon. He had married a girl from the merchant class, rather than the aristocracy, and there would always be people who looked down on Lady Rufford for her background.

Ivy's own background was far more scandalous than her aunt's, but no one outside the family knew the true story, and Ivy hoped to keep it that way. Lord and Lady Rufford had raised her from infancy and lavished both their affection and their worldly goods on her. The least she could do was keep from humiliating them by allowing anyone to learn the sordid tale.

"Do you think the earl's younger brother will be there?" Rose asked. "Mr. Selwyn? I am looking forward to meeting him."

Ivy turned her head toward her cousin and smiled, knowing perfectly well why Rose looked forward to meeting young Mr. Selwyn. They made friends in Bath last spring who knew Mr. Selwyn and sang his praises. Rose had begun building some rather foolish castles in the air about him, despite never having met him.

"I don't know. He may be there. He may not. But I do know there will be plenty of young people. You have nothing to worry about." Lady Rufford smiled benevolently at Rose. Then she turned her eyes toward Ivy. "You too, my dear," she said affectionately. "I hope you meet some young people to your liking."

Ivy snorted. Unlike her debutante cousin, Ivy was not on the hunt for a husband. "I will be five-and-twenty in less than a week," she reminded her aunt. "I am a confirmed spinster."

"Nonsense!" Lady Rufford shook her head briskly, setting her golden ringlets dancing. Her hair, much the same color as Rose's, was only lightly touched by white. No one looking at her would guess she had a nineteen-year-old daughter. "You are a gem of a girl, and I know some gentleman will recognize that."

"Thank you, Aunt Rufford." Ivy smiled, not wanting to cause a quarrel. Her aunt and uncle refused to admit that Ivy would probably never marry. It was as if their affection blinded them to all the things that made her ineligible to be the wife of a gentleman. Ivy, on the other hand, had realized this before she even left the schoolroom. She accepted that her lot in life would be to comfort and support the rest of her family while trying to minimize the scandal of her birth.

Since she did not share Rose's matrimonial aspirations, Ivy did not look forward to this house party the way Rose did. Nor did she particularly care to spend three weeks away from home with strangers who might or might not make for congenial company. The house party appealed to her only in so far as it gave her a chance to explore a new part of the country. She had never been to Lancashire before. While her aunt and uncle had napped, Ivy stayed awake during most of the day's journey in order to drink in the unfamiliar landscape.

The carriage pulled up in front of the grand entrance to the house, and a groom got down to help the ladies out. Before they could do more than look at the castle, the door opened, and a line of servants came out to receive them. At the center, in front of the door, stood a man whose dark hair had begun to silver at the temples. He stood only a little over average height for a man, but something about the set of his shoulders and the expression on his face gave him a commanding presence.

"Ah, there's Inglewhite," Lord Rufford whispered. He led the way to the earl.

"Rufford! Well met!" Lord Inglewhite stepped forward to clasp Uncle Rufford's hand. "My lady," he added, looking at Aunt Rufford, "You don't seem to have aged a bit since last I saw you."

Aunt Rufford laughed. "Flatterer! A woman with a daughter of marrying age cannot pretend to be young anymore. Save your compliments for the young ladies of the party."

Lord Inglewhite turned his head in the direction of the two younger women.

"May I present Miss Rufford and Miss Burnley?" Lord Rufford said. "You have, of course, met my daughter, but not since she was a child, I think. Miss Burnley is her cousin and my ward."

Rose curtseyed very prettily. Ivy followed not *quite* as gracefully. Her legs still felt half-asleep after hours of carriage travel. *Former ward*, Ivy thought, smiling to herself. Legally, Uncle Rufford had ceased to be her guardian when she turned twenty-one. But she knew that in his mind the relationship was a permanent one.

"Very pleased to meet you, ladies," the earl said graciously. "But please, come in and warm yourselves by the fire. The day is cold." The sharp wind gusting about the top of the hill underscored his words.

As they entered the castle, Ivy saw she had been right about the Great Hall. A small foyer led into a room with a high ceiling and an enormous fireplace that took up most of one wall. Settles and armchairs were drawn in front of the hearth, and the travelers hurried to the fire to warm up. Lord Rufford and Lord Inglewhite discussed the state of the roads and the chances of snow. Lady Rufford fussed over Rose, who caught cold easily. And Ivy, left alone for a moment, looked about the hall.

What she saw disappointed her. After her first glimpse of Selwyn Castle, she had expected medieval banners hanging on the walls, suits of armor, and other trappings of a distant past. Instead, the room had been modernized within the last century. It still boasted stone flagging rather than tiles on the floor, but it had been paneled with oak. Instead of rusty armor or fading tapestries, family portraits hung on the walls.

Ivy approached one of the portraits, which showed a pair of boys standing outside with a pony. The pony caught her eye immediately. It was a round, jolly-looking dappled gray, and the painter had captured a spark of mischief in its eyes. But who, she wondered, were the two boys? Both were dark haired and blue eyed, though the elder was lean and tall and the younger built on more stocky lines.

"You are interested in artwork, Miss Burnley?" While Ivy had been distracted by the painting, Lord Inglewhite had approached without her noticing. He stood behind her, a little to the left.

She looked over her shoulder at him, startled. Because her

uncle was a baron, she had met members of the aristocracy many times before, but conversing with an earl still made her nervous. Being only a little taller than Ivy, Lord Inglewhite did not loom over her, but there was nevertheless something imposing about his presence.

"It is not so much that I am interested in art as that I am interested in ponies," she explained. "And then I wondered who the children were." She liked children *almost* as well as ponies, but she did not want to admit that. Lord Inglewhite might think she was on the market for a husband and a family.

"Ah." He smiled and pointed at the taller of the two boys. "That is my older brother, Robert. The previous Lord Inglewhite. And the younger boy is me, of course. This was taken before my younger brother was born, so I must have been no more than seven. The pony's name was Ganymede." His smile widened, showing a glimpse of straight teeth. "He was a stubborn little thing, but we loved him dearly."

"I am sure you did." Ivy smiled back. "I named my pony Merlin, but he was such a sweet, tame little gelding that I do not think he ever lived up to his magical name." She thought nostalgically of the way Merlin would refuse to take fences, or to gallop, or indeed to move faster than a dignified trot, most of the time. "He is still alive, but has been put out to pasture." His joints hurt too much for him to be ridden, even if there had been any young children in the family to ride him.

"Are you fond of riding, then?" Lord Inglewhite asked her.

"Oh, yes," she said at once. "I do not hunt, but I have a very sweet-tempered hack named Chanticleer. My cousin and I love to ride about the country together." Though Rose did not like to ramble as far and wide as Ivy did, nor did she like to stay out in the sun for very long, lest she develop freckles. Ivy did not mind a few freckles.

"If the weather allows, I should show you the trail along the river," he suggested. "The woods are still lovely, even with all the leaves fallen."

"I would like that." Ivy's smile fell as she remembered, too late, that she had promised her aunt she would do her best to help chaperone Rose. "If my duties allow it. I am here mostly to chaperone my cousin, you know."

Ivy glanced over her shoulder, looking for Rose. She found her cousin quickly, because Rose's golden curls shone in the firelight as she talked to a young man with auburn hair—a color very close to Ivy's own hair, in fact.

"Surely your aunt can look after her own daughter?" Lord Inglewhite sounded surprised by the arrangement.

Ivy turned her gaze back to him and shook her head. "My aunt's health does not permit her to be as active as she likes. Since I am a spinster myself, I help chaperone my cousin."

Aunt Rufford's migraines often prevented her from accompanying Rose, particularly when Rose chose to walk, ride, or ramble outside. Bright sunlight sometimes triggered one of Aunt Rufford's headaches. Over the last few years, Ivy had become used to stepping in and helping with her aunt's duties. She hoped such assistance demonstrated her gratitude towards the relatives who had raised her.

To her surprise, Lord Inglewhite chuckled. "A spinster, are you? At your age? What are you, all of three-and-twenty?" A smile teased at the corners of his mouth, eliminating any possible offense.

Ivy scowled at him. "You should never ask a lady her age, sir. But since you asked, I will be five-and-twenty on Christmas Eve." Not being particularly vain, she saw no reason to make a secret of her age.

"My guess was close enough." He shrugged his shoulders, a smile lingering at the corners of his eyes and mouth. "As I am already an old man of seven-and-thirty, you will forgive me for thinking you are still young, Miss Burnley."

Ivy did not know what to say in response. She thought the earl wrong on two accounts. First, most gentlemen preferred younger brides, and women of the aristocracy tended to marry in their late teens or early twenties. Once a woman reached five-and-twenty, many people considered her an old maid. And Ivy did not expect to marry anyone, though her age was the least of her reasons.

At the same time, she thought the earl wrong to call himself "old." As with so many aspects of life, the standards for aging differed for men. A man of seven-and-thirty was still considered to be in the prime of his life, and many women would find Lord Inglewhite attractive, even with silvered hair. Maybe *because* of his silvered hair. But she could not tell Lord Inglewhite that. She did not want him to think she was trying to flirt with him.

She was relieved when the housekeeper—an elderly woman dressed in black silk—approached and interrupted their conversation. "Ladies, may I show you to your rooms? You will want to dress for dinner soon."

"We keep country hours here," Lord Inglewhite explained to his guests. "We dine at six."

"Then we had better hurry," Lady Rufford agreed, and the new arrivals followed the housekeeper to their rooms.

Ivy had expected to share a room with Rose, as they often did when they traveled. But to her surprise, they were each given their own bedroom. Selwyn Castle must be bigger than it had looked at first glance if it had so many guest rooms.

"This house party is going to be so much fun!" Rose squealed and clapped her hands with glee. "Did you see that good-looking gentleman with auburn hair? That is Lord Francis Bracknell. He has the bluest eyes I have ever seen! He is the vicar at St. John's, in Ingleton. He says he will dine here often during the party, even though he is not staying at the castle."

"He looked young to be a clergyman." Ivy had not gotten a good look at him, but she thought him close to her own age. But he must be at least four-and-twenty if he were already in orders.

"Yes, this is his first living. We will get to hear him preach on Sunday!"

Privately, Ivy wondered if so young a cleric could possibly be a good preacher. No doubt he had been well educated, but had he even seen enough of life to have material for his sermons? She kept her doubts to herself, though. Rose already seemed disposed to admire Lord Francis.

They met the rest of the guests in the drawing room before dinner. Ivy quickly realized that the party was unbalanced: there were more unmarried men than unmarried women. The only girl of marrying age other than Rose was Arabella Canning, daughter of Sir Michael Canning. She was accompanied by her brother, Joshua, who looked like he might still be a university student.

The auburn-haired clergyman had a brother, too, though the two men did not much resemble each other. Lord Crowthorne was dark haired, dark eyed, and taller than Lord Francis. He seemed more reserved than his amiable younger brother, and there was a haughty cast to his expression. Ivy was not sure she liked him.

But she did like Lord Francis and Joshua Canning, both of whom sat next to her at dinner. Rose sat on the other side of Lord Francis and looked pleased with her position. Ivy half-expected to be ignored in favor of her younger cousin, but Lord Francis followed etiquette and divided his conversation evenly between his two partners.

Rather to her surprise, Ivy enjoyed her dinner table conversations. She often had difficulty conversing with strangers, but not this time. Lord Francis spoke to her of books and Christmas carols. Mr. Canning, who had visited Selwyn Castle before, talked about horses, curricles, and the best rides in the area. Both subjects interested her, and the dinner hours passed far more quickly than she would ever have imagined.

In truth, Ivy had not expected to enjoy this house party very much. She was a creature of habit and would far rather have celebrated the holidays at Rufford Manor, as the family usually did. She liked being surrounded by familiar settings and familiar faces. She liked the aging vicar of St. Sebastian's parish, even though he preached virtually the same Christmas sermon year after year. And she loved the holiday party Lord Rufford always held for his tenants. It gave her a rare chance to mingle socially with the daughters of local farmers.

At home, Ivy would know what to expect, because things had always been done the same way at Rufford Manor for as long as she could remember. She would know exactly how the goose would be seasoned, and what would be in the pudding. She could predict which songs the carolers were likely to sing when they visited the Manor. She even knew which ghost stories people were likely to tell around the hearth on Christmas Eve. All of those things, taken together, were a large part of what Christmas meant to her.

But she had no idea what to expect at Selwyn Castle. She did not know how the Selwyn family celebrated Christmas, how the cook stuffed the goose, or what songs the carolers in Lancashire might sing. She did not even know if carolers *would* call at the Castle. For all she knew, it might be too far from the village for people to make the trek. And she would far rather have celebrated the religious feast of Christmas at her own familiar parish. It would not be the same attending a strange church!

She went to bed that night with mixed feelings. On the one hand, she longed for her own room and her own familiar bed. Though this bed felt comfortable, it felt just strange enough to make it hard for her to sleep. On the other hand, Ivy could not deny that she'd had fun after dinner, when the guests played "Forfeits" to hilarious results. Perhaps the party would not be so bad after all.

Chapter Two

*E*VERYTHING WILL BE *fine*, Richard told himself as he waited for the Rufford family to clamber out of their carriage. He would have felt more comfortable if his friend Downing were there, with his three unmarried sisters. The sisters would have helped balance the guest list, which would be uneven if Richard's younger brother attended the house party, as he had promised. Downing hosted country house parties every summer, so he could have advised Richard. But the Downing family had been struck with scarlet fever, confining them to their own estate for the holidays. Richard would not have Downing's advice.

He was not precisely alone, because his aunt served as the official hostess of the party. But Aunt Agatha had always been of a retiring nature, never circulating much in society. She could inform Richard of details about past house parties at Selwyn Castle, but she had never served as hostess before. Moreover, she was nearly seventy-five years old and not very active. She would be of limited practical assistance.

Lord Rufford's arrival relieved Richard of some of the stress of the last few weeks. He'd known Rufford for many years, though the baron was closer in age to Richard's late older brother. The two had become closer during last spring's parliamentary sessions. But Rufford did not usually bring his family with him to London, so the young ladies in the family were veritable strangers to Richard. And good lord, Miss Rufford had changed completely! The last time Richard had seen her, she'd been an awkward schoolgirl. Now she was an elegant young lady whom he would not have recognized if he passed her in the street.

Richard was not sure he had ever met Rufford's young niece. Surely, he would have remembered Miss Burnley for the sake of her striking hair color? Her rich auburn locks kept catching his eye as the family entered the Great Hall. It drew him to her side to chat about the portrait of himself and his brother with the pony. Goodness, he had not thought about Ganymede in years, though he really had been a marvelous pony. Much better than the flighty mare Richard had been given when he outgrew him.

He was still thinking about horseback riding and hoping the weather would cooperate with a ride along the river trail when his valet came in to dress him. Then disaster struck. "My lord," Saunders said, "did you by any chance move the sapphire stickpin? It is not in its box."

"What?" Richard had been peering into his cheval glass to check the hang of his topcoat, but he immediately swung his head around to stare at Saunders. "I haven't touched that pin. You put it away properly last time I wore it, didn't you?" He thought he remembered as much, but he had not worn that stickpin for weeks.

"I most certainly did!" Indignation filled Saunders' voice. "I cleaned it and put it back in the case after you dined at the vicarage. But the case is empty. See?" He held up the empty wooden box as proof. There could be no denying that the pin was gone.

Richard wrinkled his brow, feeling both anxious and confused. "Perhaps it was merely mislaid? It must be about here somewhere." He was more worried than he let on, though. That stickpin was his favorite piece of jewelry. His mother had given it to him as a gift when he was ordained, saying the pale blue sapphire matched his eyes. She died not long afterward, carried off by a raging infection (caused by a cat scratch, of all things). Richard could have lost almost any of his other possessions without experiencing nearly as much of a pang.

"Perhaps." Saunders said nothing more, but he sniffed and turned up his nose as if to suggest that *he* would never lose a piece of jewelry.

"Just use the plain gold pin," Richard told his valet, "and we will look for the missing pin later." He had enough on his plate to deal with without worrying about missing jewelry.

When Richard went downstairs to confer with his butler about dinner, things got worse. Gibson informed him that a few items from the silver service had gone missing.

"Perhaps we should interrogate the new scullery maid," Gibson suggested. "This is her first time in service, and she came without a reference. We only took her on because one of the housemaids vouched for her."

Richard sighed. He felt certain that any interrogation would terrify the maid, who could be no more than fifteen years old. "Could the silverware have been misplaced?"

Gibson drew himself to his highest height (which was not very high) and said: "In this household, my lord, we do not misplace the silver."

Gibson's suggestion of a thief among the kitchen staff seemed unlikely. Why would anyone steal fish forks, of all things? The individual items could not be worth much. Of course, his sapphire stickpin had also gone missing, but that could not have been filched by the new scullery maid. She would have no reason to come to that part of the house.

But Richard could not rule out entirely the possibility of a thief. Upper housemaids would have access to the bedrooms, since they were responsible for cleaning them. They might also have errands that took them into the kitchen. Could one of them have run into some kind of money trouble? A debt that had to be repaid, for example? Or medical expenses for a family member? Desperate situations could make people behave in unexpected ways.

"I am sure it will turn up," Richard insisted. He did not want to encourage the idea of a thieving servant. All it would take would be a few rumors, and then everyone in the household would suspect everyone else. Such an atmosphere would not be conducive to anyone's comfort or wellbeing.

Gibson did not scowl in response. He maintained the impassive expression required of butlers. But Richard thought he read faint signs of disapproval in the butler's face.

"Let us hope they do. The silversmith who made that set in your father's time retired years ago, so it will not be possible to replace the pieces." Gibson delivered this information with the same gloomy solemnity with which he might have announced a death in the family.

Richard, who did not care one bit about silver, was almost tempted to laugh. But he controlled his voice as best he could as he reassured Gibson. "If need be, we will buy a new silver service." It might be expensive, but good butlers were hard to find, and Richard would pay a good deal to keep Gibson content.

"Very well, sir." Gibson inclined his head and exited, leaving Richard to silently weigh his next actions. Should he warn the guests that there might be a thief in the castle? He did not want to unduly alarm anyone, but the guests might deserve a warning. They might look after their valuables more carefully if they knew things were going missing lately. And they might keep their eyes open for anything suspicious.

Richard silently went back and forth over that question at dinner that night. In fact, he grew so distracted that he absent-mindedly told the Marchioness of Reading he liked goose stuffed with chesterfields, rather than chestnuts. It took some verbal finessing to backtrack from that malapropism. People were going to think him absent-minded if he did not pay better attention.

In the end, he resolved to wait and see rather than publicly revealing his suspicions. If more objects disappeared, he would have to take action. Then he would warn the guests, and perhaps search the servants' quarters. But he very much hoped it would not come to that.

As it was, dinner that night presented its own anxieties. There had been a great shake-up in the kitchen during the weeks preceding the house party. Monsieur Durand, who had ruled the castle kitchen for two decades, had decided to return to France now that the war was over. He gave only two weeks' notice, which did not allow time to hire a replacement of the same caliber.

Richard did not believe in poaching servants from his neighbors, but he broke his own rule and enticed Squire Anderson's head cook to leave Greyfriar's Hall and come to work at Selwyn Castle. She could only cook English cuisine, but she was far more experienced than the castle's assistant cook, who was not yet ready to take over management of so large a kitchen. At least, so Mrs. Cadwallader and Gibson said, and Richard treated their word as law. Both the housekeeper and the butler had served at Selwyn since his father's time, and they knew far more about running the castle than Richard did.

To compound the disaster of losing Monsieur Durand, Richard had casually mentioned the defection in a letter to his brother, Rowland. Rowland wrote back to say that he might stay in London for the holidays after all. He did not trust Mrs. Mason's cooking and thought his club could provide him with better meals. Richard found this positively infuriating. The whole reason for the house party was to help Rowland find an eligible young lady to court! What was the point of inviting all these guests if Rowland intended to stay in London for the holidays? Richard had no desire to host a Christmas party for his own sake.

But it was too late to cancel the house party. Whether or not Rowland showed up, Richard would have to entertain nearly a dozen guests with only Aunt Agatha's sporadic assistance. After dinner, he exerted himself to be a cheerful, helpful host. Fortunately, the guests were disposed to enjoy themselves. Rose Rufford suggested a game of Forfeits, and young Mr. Canning enthusiastically seconded her.

Mr. Canning collected forfeits from each of the guests: a silk handkerchief from Lady Reading, a pocket watch from Richard, and little trinkets from the other guests. Meanwhile, Lord Francis Bracknell called for paper and a pencil so that he could jot down all the possible forfeits. Richard was rather taken aback by some of the suggestions. Was this really how people played the game in the fashionable world? The last time he played Forfeits, he had been a child. Most of the forfeits had involved convoluted gymnastic exercises or reciting a line of poetry backwards. Richard worried that some of *these* forfeits were unseemly, to say the least.

No one else seemed to have any reservations, though. Even the very dignified Lady Reading got to her feet and attempted to imitate a chicken scratching for food in order to reclaim her bracelet. Miss Burnley gamely sang "Rule Britannia" while balancing an empty bottle on her head, and Sir Michael Canning tried his hardest to stand on his head, laughing heartily despite his failure.

When it was Richard's turn, the slip of paper he drew out of the hat commanded him to describe the worst punishment he had received in school. He could still remember it clearly: he had fallen asleep during chapel and gotten soundly thrashed as a result. He could tell that the audience was disappointed by this story, but what could he do? Unlike his brother Rowland, Richard had always been a dutiful child. He collected his pocket watch, relieved that he hadn't had to do anything too humiliating.

His composure was promptly shaken, because the next person to draw from the hat was Miss Canning, a shy girl who wore her dark blonde tresses in a simple knot at the back of her head, with no curls or hair ornaments. Her face flushed prettily when she read aloud the forfeit she drew, demanding that she kiss a member of the opposite sex.

Richard wondered if he ought to intervene. It did not seem right to force such a reserved young lady to kiss a gentleman. But before he could make up his mind, she began walking slowly around the room. The chairs had been arranged in a rough circle so that everyone could easily watch all the forfeits being performed. Miss Canning walked the circle, studying the different gentlemen. She paused for a moment before Lord Francis, then blushed and hurried past.

When Miss Canning reached Richard, she paused again. He expected her to move on. Instead, she leaned down and dropped a soft kiss on his cheek. Her blush deepened as she scurried back to her empty chair. Richard clapped a hand to his cheek, startled, while everyone else laughed. Miss Canning claimed the brooch that had been taken from her, and the next partygoer drew a forfeit.

Truth be told, Richard felt rather alarmed by such attention, though he tried to hide his alarm with boisterous laughter. That night, after Saunders had left, Richard lay in bed and worried about the kiss. It was just a game, right? Miss Canning wasn't trying to flirt with him, was she? He hoped it would be clear that *he* was not on the hunt for a wife. Wasn't it obvious that a single man of his age must be a confirmed bachelor? Even if he had wanted to marry, Miss Canning was far too young for him. She could not be much more than twenty.

As it happened, Richard had no intention of marrying anyone at all, regardless of age. His life as a bachelor suited him very well.

He had briefly reconsidered the matter of matrimony last year, when Robert's death unexpectedly made Richard the new earl. He had wondered then if it was his duty to marry, little though he felt inclined to do so. Certainly, his sister-in-law began talking about his need to choose a countess. Probably other members of the Selwyn family shared Sophia's opinion.

But with a younger brother in good health, Richard need not worry about producing an heir. Let Rowland marry and set up his nursery! All Rowland needed was a little push in the right direction, a few introductions to the right people, and the perfect environment for courtship. Hence, the Christmas party.

Everyone knew house parties lent themselves to matchmaking. Richard had certainly seen it work at the houses of his friends. Why shouldn't it work at Selwyn Castle, too?

Rowland spent most of his time in London, but he occupied himself with sporting events and (Richard feared) gambling houses rather than attending Almack's and the private balls and parties of the *ton* where he might meet a prospective bride. But Rowland would turn thirty on his next birthday, and it was time for him to settle down. Even Rowland had admitted as much when last he visited the castle. So, Richard had planned this house party to give his brother a nudge towards matrimony, inviting guests with an eye toward families with daughters of marrying age.

Miss Canning seemed too shy to suit someone as social as Rowland, but Richard had hoped one of the Misses Downing would catch Rowland's eye. Damn the scarlet fever for ruining those plans! At this point, Richard reminded himself that he was not the primary sufferer of the fever, and he said a quick prayer for healing for the Downing family. Then he returned his thoughts to the problem of Rowland's matrimonial chances.

Even with the Misses Downing out of the picture, all was not lost. If Rowland would condescend to come home for a visit, perhaps the very pretty Miss Rufford would catch his eye. Or her cousin, the girl with the lovely hair and the soulful brown eyes. Richard had no idea whether Miss Burnley had a dowry to match Miss Rufford's, but Rowland had inherited a competence from their mother, and he did not need to marry an heiress.

But if Rowland stayed in London, all Richard's matchmaking plans would be for naught. Worse, everyone would assume that Richard was on the hunt for a bride.

Once, admittedly, Richard had thought to marry. He had made it to the age of seven-and-twenty without bruising his heart, only to fall madly and (as it turned out) hopelessly in love with the dashing, stylish Barbara Dixon. Barbara encouraged his suit, flirting with him, dancing with him, and even letting him kiss her beneath the stars. Richard had been certain that a lifetime of matrimonial bliss lay before him.

But when he proposed to Barbara, she tearfully told him that she could not return his feelings. A few weeks later, she became engaged to marry a much older man whose most attractive feature seemed to be his title. Evidently, Barbara preferred being Lady Morgan to simple Mrs. Selwyn.

Crushed, he threw himself into his work. For a few years, he ignored all the eager young misses who would have been happy to marry the younger son of an earl. Then Amabel Henderson changed his mind. She caught Richard's attention not with witty repartee or dazzling dress, but with her stalwart commitment to charity. She founded a lady's sewing circle dedicated to making children's clothes for all the Sunday school scholars. She taught a Sunday school class as well. And if a tenant on the Henderson estate were ill or injured, she would be found on hand, bringing soup, medicine, or other comforts.

That latter habit was what brought about her demise. Only a few weeks after Amabel joyfully accepted Richard's proposal of marriage, she contracted scarlet fever while tending a sick child. It spread throughout the Henderson household, and despite the best medical treatment, both Amabel and her father died of the illness.

While Richard lost a fiancée, Mrs. Henderson lost everything. The Hendersons had no sons, so their estate devolved to a nephew who was quite eager to take control of the property. He graciously allowed Mrs. Henderson the use of the dower house. There she eked out a lonely existence on a too-small income. Richard sent her a ham or a haunch of venison when he could, but nothing could replace the loss of her husband and only child.

After this second matrimonial disappointment, Richard resolved to remain single. Whatever comfort and affection he might have lost by that decision was more than compensated for by his freedom from heartache and domestic strife. All he wanted now was to ensure the continuation of the family name by giving his brother a nudge towards matrimony. If Rowland remained in London, this entire house party was pointless. And now, Miss Canning's kiss suggested that his guests had drawn the wrong conclusions about Richard's own matrimonial intentions—or rather, the lack thereof.

Somehow, Richard had to play the part of the host without giving any of the eligible young ladies false encouragement. As if that weren't challenge enough, he also had to keep a look out for a possible thief among the servants. If any more silverware disappeared, Gibson might be inconsolable. Well, Richard had learned his lesson. Next time he wanted company over the holidays, he would accept his sister-in-law's invitation to spend the holiday with them. This house party was clearly a colossal mistake.

Chapter Three

December 20

THE FIRST FEW days of the party passed promisingly enough. When the weather allowed, the horsey members of the party rode about the park or along nearby country lanes. When it rained, they played parlor games instead. On Friday night they shuffled the furniture around in the Great Hall and held a dance. Ivy had not expected this, but she was delighted. She loved dancing.

She danced the first dance with young Mr. Canning. He was very polite, but a little clumsy. She guessed he might not have had much experience dancing yet, being so young. At least he apologized charmingly every time he made a misstep. Still, she felt a little relieved when their set ended and they separated to find new partners.

After that set ended, Lord Francis asked her to stand up with him. "Do clergymen dance?" she asked Lord Francis. She had never seen the vicar of St. Sebastian's dancing. But then, he must be at least seventy, so perhaps his health did not permit it.

He shrugged. "Perhaps some clergymen frown on dancing, but I see nothing wrong with a country dance. I do not waltz, though, so as not to scandalize the more conservative members of my parish." His eyes crinkled, inviting her to smile with him.

"They will probably not have waltzing here, anyway," Ivy guessed. Waltzing was more popular in London than in the countryside, though its appearance at the king's birthday ball last summer suggested the dance had finally become acceptable at the highest levels of society.

But Ivy was promptly proven wrong, because the musician struck up a waltz. True to his word, Lord Francis sat this one out. Ivy guessed that she would be left on the sidelines, too, partners being limited. Lord Crowthorne stood up with Arabella Canning, and Mr. Canning hovered near Rose, looking like he intended to ask her to dance. The older gentlemen who were dancing seemed already to have chosen partners, too. Ivy took a seat, prepared to watch the dancers and wait for the next country dance.

"Do you not waltz, Miss Burnley?" She lifted her eyes and saw the Earl of Inglewhite, looking very elegant in the simple black and white of his evening attire.

"Oh, I love to waltz!" she exclaimed. Then she blushed, because that sounded as if she were fishing for an invitation to dance. She did not expect an invitation from this quarter. So far, the earl had ignored the young women of the party to dance only with older, married women.

But he overturned all her expectations by asking "In that case, would you do me the honor of this dance?"

Ivy stood up and let him take her by the hand, but she was so surprised that she could say nothing for the first few minutes of the dance. She had not waltzed in some time, and it took her a few steps to remember the rhythm of the dance.

Fortunately, Lord Inglewhite was a better dance partner than Mr. Canning had been. The partygoers performed the more restrained version of the waltz, in which the gentleman held the lady's hand rather than putting his hand on her waist. Two layers of gloves separated Ivy's hand from Lord Inglewhite's. Even so, the longer they danced, the more distracting Lord Inglewhite's touch became. She felt far more aware of him—his touch, his presence, his proximity—than she had with any of her previous dance partners.

He remained quiet, too. As the silence stretched out, she felt increasingly sorry for him. Clearly, he had only asked her to dance for the sake of politeness. Very likely he would have preferred to sit the dance out. He must be trying to play the part of a good host.

At last, Lord Inglewhite broke the silence. "Are you enjoying your visit, Miss Burnley?"

"Isn't that a dangerous question for a host to ask a guest? What if I told you I was not enjoying myself at all?" She smiled so he would know she meant no real complaint.

But he had a ready answer. "Then I should have to work harder to keep you entertained, of course. *Is* there anything not to your liking here?" He looked down into her eyes earnestly.

This close to him, she could see his eyes were not gray, as they initially appeared, but a light, clear blue. *Like sunlight shining through stained glass*, she thought, but immediately dismissed the thought as fanciful.

"I would have to be a very finicky guest to find anything to displease me here," Ivy assured him. "You have assembled a delightful party of houseguests, and I do not see how anyone could complain about your hospitality." She paused, not certain if she should say more. It would probably be best to leave it at that.

Somehow, he picked up on her hesitancy. "But?" he prompted. "There *is* something bothering you, isn't there?"

She shook her head. "There is nothing wrong with this party. It is just that I am a homebody at heart. I know travel is good for expanding one's mind, but I will always love home the best. And it is particularly hard being away at this time of year. I have never spent a Christmas away from home." She could not keep all of the wistfulness out of her voice.

"Have you lived all your life at Rufford Manor?" He sounded surprised.

"Nearly. My parents died in a carriage accident when I was a baby." That was a lie. Her mother died only a few years ago, of influenza. For all she knew of her father, he might still be alive. But the truth about her parentage could never be spoken. "I have lived at Rufford Manor for as long as I can remember, and I am very attached to it." That part, at least, was nothing but the truth.

"I suppose it is difficult for women to leave their homes when they marry. Men do not have to do that. At least, not eldest sons." He smiled wryly. "Younger sons who must work for a living are a different matter. But I used to be clergyman here at St. John's, so I did not have to settle far from home."

"Really?" Ivy's eyes widened with surprise. "I did not know you had a profession at all."

"My older brother inherited the title when our father died," he reminded her. "He has been gone only a year. I served as vicar in Ingleton for nearly a decade before that."

"I see." She had forgotten that he'd been a younger son. "Why did you become a clergyman rather than a barrister or an officer in the army?" She spoke without thinking, then blushed when she realized how intrusive the question might seem. His career choices were none of her business.

But he answered her anyway, seeming not to find her question impertinent. "I always had an interest in Scripture and theology. And I like being useful. A clergyman has many opportunities to help people." Then he grinned. "Of course, the fact that my father had a living in his gift was also a factor. Perhaps I would have not been so quick to seek ordination if I expected to spend many years as a poor curate."

"I suppose the life of a curate is very hard." Ivy knew curates were expected to work diligently, for little pay. They might wait for years before finding a living of their own.

"All of the professions are challenging in their own way. My younger brother read law at Gray's Inn, and I know he found the study rather dry." This time, his smile took on a distinctively rueful cast. "He has only tried a few cases."

"Will Mr. Selwyn be here this Christmas?" she asked, remembering Rose's interest in the earl's younger brother. They had been surprised (and in Rose's case, a little disappointed) to find Mr. Selwyn not in residence.

Lord Inglewhite shrugged, and his smile faded. "Rowland said he might make it, but I do not count on his presence. Perhaps it is just as well. I believe we have gentlemen enough without him. He might not like the competition." His eyes darted in the direction of Lord Crowthorne, who had been blessed with both good looks and a high position as heir to a Marquisate.

"I suppose so," Ivy agreed, "especially when there are only two eligible young misses to court." Not that matrimony was the only reason for attending a house party, of course. But Rose certainly had marriageable young men on her mind, and Ivy suspected Miss Canning did, too, for all that she was so shy.

"Only two?" He scrunched up his face, looking confused.

"Miss Rufford and Miss Canning," Ivy explained. "They are the only young ladies of marrying age."

"Ah, yes, you being at the advanced age of five-and-twenty." The earl spoke gravely, but the way the corners of his eyes crinkled suggested amusement rather than solemnity.

"I do not intend to marry," she said sharply. She knew perfectly well that her uncle and aunt still hoped she might make a match, but she had no such illusions. Ivy's only goal was to help her cousin make a good match. Being of service to the Ruffords was the only way she could imagine repaying them for the care and attention they had given her since infancy.

Some unidentifiable emotion flickered across Lord Inglewhite's face. "We are in the same boat, then. I am a confirmed bachelor myself." He sounded cheerful, so she could only assume that if she had startled him, he recovered quickly.

"Oh." Ivy hoped she hid her surprise well. She had assumed this house party was intended to help Lord Inglewhite choose a bride. Now that he held the title, he must want a wife—right? The author of *Pride and Prejudice* had certainly implied as much in the opening lines of the novel! It was a truth universally acknowledged that an unmarried earl in possession of a large castle must be in want of a wife.

"It is fun to watch other people pair off, though," Ivy added. She cast her eyes about the room and saw Rose dancing with young Mr. Canning again. Privately, she thought that an unlikely match. Mr. Canning was too young for an engagement yet. He ought at the very least take his degree before he thought of marrying.

"Yes, playing matchmaker can be rewarding. That is why I had hoped my younger brother would grace us with his presence." A hint of bitterness colored Lord Inglewhite's voice.

"Perhaps he will yet arrive," she suggested, trying to console him. It did seem rather rude of Mr. Selwyn to avoid his own brother's Christmas party. "We still have several days before Christmas."

The waltz ended before Lord Inglewhite could say anything in response. He bowed to her, she curtseyed in return, and they parted. He sat out the next dance, but Ivy danced a reel with Sir Michael Canning, who proved to be a better dancer than his son. Perhaps, she thought kindly, young Mr. Canning would improve as he aged. At present, he was rather like an unripe cheese, and as such, it was not fair to judge him.

After that lively dance, Ivy sat out to catch her breath. When Lady Canning took a seat beside her to chat, Ivy's eyes were drawn to the magnificent rubies the older woman wore. The stones were enormous; the setting graceful rather than overly ornate, as many heirloom jewels were.

Lady Canning must have seen the direction Ivy's eyes took, for she said "These are the prize jewels of the Canning family. The setting is new, but the gems have been in the family for generations."

"They look lovely with your dress," Ivy replied. Lady Canning wore a festive red velvet dress with white lace at the hem and neckline.

"You look very well this evening, too," Lady Canning said

kindly.

"Thank you." But Ivy looked down at her own white silk dress, with its Pomona green trim, and wrinkled her nose. She wished she had the freedom to wear rich colors like what the married women wore. Her aunt insisted in dressing Ivy in white or pastel colors, as if she were still a debutante. She would have looked much better had she been able to wear a vivid green or a rich purple.

She kept thinking wistfully about brightly colored evening dresses after the party broke up for the night. Once she turned five-and-twenty, would Aunt Rufford allow her to dress like a grown woman instead of a young girl? She could only hope.

But Ivy had no hope of ever owning a set of jewels like Lady Canning's rubies. She had a respectable fortune, thanks to her grandfather's generosity, but even that might not be adequate for a parure of rubies—or something better suited to her complexion. And even if she had the money, such a purchase would be too extravagant to possibly justify. Ivy knew it was foolish and worldly of her to long for such riches, but she could not help wondering what she would have looked like decked out in emeralds or diamonds.

Ivy fell asleep and dreamed of jeweled necklaces, bracelets, and hair clips. She remembered that dream three days later, when Lady Canning's maid discovered that someone had stolen the precious rubies right out of the Cannings' dressing room.

Chapter Four

THE SATURDAY BEFORE Christmas began well. Snow had fallen in the night, and for once it stuck, leaving the whole estate looking like a richly frosted cake. As Richard stared out his bedroom window, he idly wondered whether there would be cake for dessert that night. Probably not. But there would certainly be cake on Christmas day, along with the traditional plum pudding, and who knew what else. The new cook had been doing very well in her role and he trusted her to create something suitable for the occasion.

The day got even better in the late afternoon, because Rowland showed up at long last. "I thought you weren't going to make it," Richard scolded as he clapped his brother on the shoulder.

"Where's the trust?" The grin on Rowland's face suggested he was not really offended. "I promised I would attend your house party, and here I am. Have I missed all the fun?"

"Nearly." Richard shook his head in mock remonstrance. "You missed the dance on Friday, and the carolers earlier today. But we plan to play charades tonight, so you have not missed that."

"Perfect," Rowland said. "My team will win, of course."

"We shall see." Richard smiled with what he hoped was a toothy, wolfish grin. But he feared he just looked foolish.

Rowland had always bested Richard when it came to good looks. Like Richard, he had the classic Selwyn coloring—blue eyes and black hair—but he somehow exuded far more presence and charisma. Richard did not like to admit he was jealous of his younger brother . . . but he was. The young ladies of the party were about to go into transports at the sight of Rowland. Not that Richard minded, of course. Because *he* was not on the hunt for a wife. As far as Richard was concerned, Rowland could have his pick of the young ladies of the party.

Richard only hoped that the charming Miss Burnley still spared a moment to chat with him now and then. It really was a shame that none of the three young bachelors had taken a liking to her, because she was both attractive and agreeable. And yet, she would have sat out the waltz if Richard had not asked her himself! If Rowland had any sense, he would turn his attentions in her direction. But Richard harbored some doubts about his brother's good sense.

Shortly before dinner, everything went to Hades. Lady Canning came to the drawing room in tears. "Someone stole my rubies!" she wailed. "They took them right out of my room! Who could have done this?"

Richard's heart skipped a beat. Then his stomach sank. "Are you sure?" he asked hoarsely. But he knew. Oh, he knew. This was all his fault for not warning the guests about the possible thief.

"Of course, I am sure." Lady Canning sounded indignant now. "We searched the entire dressing room. Then we searched my chamber. The jewels are gone!"

"I will find them," Richard promised. He rang for Gibson, and when the butler arrived, they stepped out into the empty corridor. "It is time to search the servants' quarters," Richard said grimly.

"Very good, sir." Gibson's face looked so blank that Richard had no idea whether or not he approved.

"And I think we had better search all the guests' chambers,

too," Richard added. "But I will have to clear that with the guests."

Gibson nodded. "I believe that would make the search more acceptable below stairs."

Richard sighed. "I will talk to the guests." Making that announcement was one of the hardest things he had done over the entire course of the house party; perhaps one of the hardest things he had done since inheriting the title. To his surprise, though, no one protested his proposal.

"It will be a show of good faith if we allow our rooms to be searched," Sir Michael Canning said. "I support you, Inglewhite."

Richard looked next at Lord Crowthorne, who was known for being rather temperamental. That gentleman shrugged elegantly. "I have nothing to hide," he announced. "You are most welcome to search my room, if doing so will console the staff." After those two gentlemen set the lead, the other guests all followed suit.

Richard himself conducted the search of the guests' chambers, accompanied by Mrs. Cadwallader (who knew the guest rooms better than anyone) and Sir Michael Canning, who was primarily there in the capacity of a witness. They uncovered an unexpected toupée, some scurrilous French novels, and a surprisingly large packet of biscuits the Marchioness of Reading had hidden in her wardrobe.

They did not find any of the missing objects. The only truly unexpected surprise was the dead mouse found under one of the beds. The deceased rodent did not show signs of any injuries, so its cause of death would forever be unknown. Not that anyone cared! Mrs. Cadwallader rang for a maid to dispose of it.

When Richard conferred with Gibson after dinner, he discovered that none of the missing items had been found in the servants' quarters, either. Nothing more scandalous had been discovered than some pornographic prints hidden under the second footman's bed. That might be distressing on a moral level, but it was certainly not criminal.

"Perhaps the thief did not hide the jewels in his bedroom," Gibson suggested delicately.

"Of course, he wouldn't hide them there." Richard felt exceedingly foolish for not having realized that. If the thief had any intelligence at all, he (or she) would have hidden the jewels somewhere accessible to other people, too. That way, even if the jewels were found, the thief's identity would remain a secret. "We will have to search the entire castle from top to bottom." His whole body slumped as he considered the enormity of the task.

"Yes, sir." If Gibson shared Richard's dismay, he hid it well.

Richard sighed. "I suppose we will begin tomorrow. Gibson, I leave you and Mrs. Cadwallader in charge of the investigation." Out of all the castle's staff, he trusted them the most. He would stake his life that neither of *them* would commit such a crime. But there were other servants whom he did not know well enough to vouch for.

The guests were unhappy about the results of the search, or rather the lack of results. They huddled about the drawing room, talking in whispers. The plan for charades after dinner had been forgotten. No one was in the mood for games tonight.

"Ladies and gentlemen, I think it might be best if I sent for a Bow Street Runner," Richard announced. The guests murmured, but Richard could not tell if it was an angry murmur, an anxious one, or a pleased one. "That is," he qualified, "if a Runner can be persuaded to travel so far in winter." The poor condition of the roads and the possibility of winter storms made such journeys difficult.

"I don't much fancy having a Runner about the house, poking into things," Aunt Agatha said. She'd spent the whole conversation sitting quietly in her chair, looking as calm as ever, but the quaver in her voice now suggested that she had been shaken by the crime. "Isn't there someone more genteel we might consult first?"

We already tried having gentlemen search for the jewels! Richard bit his lip to keep from arguing with his aunt.

"You could try the local constable first," suggested Sir Michael Canning. "He at least would be more familiar with the family."

"An excellent idea." Richard once again wished he had thought of it himself.

Though, now he thought about it, the village of Ingleton did not have a constable—only a pair of night watchmen. But he resolved to send for the local magistrate, it being his responsibility to investigate crimes. Unfortunately, the magistrate was Squire Anderson, who might still be miffed because Richard had lured his cook away from him before the holidays. Richard cringed at the thought of asking him for help. But what else could he do? At least Squire Anderson would satisfy Aunt Agatha's desire for a "genteel" investigator.

Squire Anderson answered the summons not long after breakfast the next day. He conferred with Richard, then with Gibson and Mrs. Cadwallader. He nodded his head and stroked his chin thoughtfully. But he did not sound optimistic about their chances of recovering the jewels.

"They could have been taken by anyone in the house, and they could have been put anywhere," he reminded Richard. "People always suspect the servants, but a young gentleman or even a young lady who runs up gaming debts may steal to pay those debts."

Richard sighed. "You are very likely right." It seemed foolish to pay so-called "debts of honor" through such a dishonorable action. But then, he thought gambling itself was foolishness at best, and sinfulness at worst. Perhaps he was not the right person to ask about etiquette concerning gambling debts. "But not all of the guests were here when the fish forks and pie servers disappeared," he reminded Squire Anderson. "The Cannings and the Bracknells had arrived, but not the Ruffords."

"Then you can probably remove the Rufford family and their servants from the list of suspects," Squire Anderson agreed. "But no one else can be ruled out."

At least that was something, Richard supposed. Not that he would really have suspected Rufford. But it could have been one of his servants. Or even—though Richard hated to entertain the thought—one of the young ladies of his party. Neither Miss Rufford nor Miss Burnley seemed at all likely to have run up gambling debts, but one never knew. Even the primmest, most proper outward persona might harbor unsavory secrets.

Chapter Five

Sunday, December 24

CHRISTMAS EVE DAWNED bright and clear. The snow had melted away, unfortunately, but that allowed those guests willing to brave the cold to take a winter walk in the afternoon, rather than being stuck in the house after returning from Sunday services. They walked through the formal gardens and into the wilderness, where the gravel walkway was not too muddy.

At the beginning of the walk, Richard moved back and forth between different clusters of guests, listening to their conversations rather than joining in. Miss Rufford walked with Lord Francis on one hand and Mr. Canning on the other, leaving her cousin to trail behind, left out of the conversation.

She ought not be neglected that way! Miss Burnley was an excellent conversationalist, as Richard had already discovered. One of the young gentlemen ought to be walking beside her. Well, perhaps Richard could make up for their neglect. He might not be on the hunt for a wife, but nothing prevented him from keeping a charming young lady company during a stroll through the grounds. He slowed down to walk beside her.

"Enjoying the walk, Miss Burnley?"

She glanced up at him and smiled. "Yes, it is good to get out of the house, even if the wind is nippy."

"Indeed." Richard wracked his brains, trying to think of something witty he could say. But though he rummaged through his head frantically, he came up empty handed. What had happened to his powers of cognition today? Usually, he found it easy to talk to Miss Burnley. As he pondered, he failed to pay attention to his surroundings—with disastrous results.

"Blast!" his companion exclaimed.

That sound brought Richard back down to earth. To be precise, he stopped woolgathering and found himself standing in the middle of a deep puddle of water. Worse, Miss Burnley had trustingly followed him right into the puddle, if "puddle" was the right word. It looked more like a miniature pond created by a combination of poor landscaping and heavy precipitation.

"I seem to have led you astray." He wrinkled his nose as he took in the messy situation. "Are you quite all right?" She stood ankle deep in muddy water, staring down at her boots with dismay.

"Does it get much deeper?" she asked anxiously. "These boots are not very high. I am afraid water will get in over the tops."

Richard studied the temporary pond. Then he looked at Miss Burnley's half boots. They were a fetching shade of green and looked well-made, but she was right: they were not high enough to allow her to walk through the puddle. Already water had nearly reached the tops.

"Will you allow me to assist you?" he offered.

Her eyes widened. "Assist me how?"

"I could lift you over the deepest part of the puddle," he explained. "That way, you would not have to go out of your way to walk around." The puddle extended several yards in each direction. Walking around would be more time consuming than walking through. Already, most of the other walkers had gotten well ahead of them. They must all have had better boots!

"Yes, that is a good idea," she said doubtfully.

Richard stepped closer to her, then started to panic. What

was he thinking? He supposed he had remembered walks where he helped his cousins or nieces over a stile or a ditch. Nothing could be more natural than to give a child a boost when needed. But Miss Burnley was not a child, and he was not her relative. She was a young lady and he was an unmarried man. There was no proper way for him to carry her over a puddle.

Heat flushed his face as Richard realized what a predicament he had stepped into. But it would be more awkward to change his mind now, wouldn't it? He had offered to help Miss Burnley, and it would be ungentlemanly to go back on his word.

So he gingerly put one hand on each side of Miss Burnley's waist and lifted her a few inches off the ground. What he had failed to consider was that in order to carry her without risking injury to himself, he had to hold her close to his own body. *Too close.*

It was not the first time Richard had come into physical contact with Miss Burnley. He had danced with her a few nights ago, mostly because he could not bear to see so likeable a woman sitting out a dance while younger girls found partners. He had enjoyed their waltz, but it had not particularly moved him, either emotionally or physically.

This was something else entirely. This time, he could not avoid noticing her proximity. He could, in fact, feel each breath she took. Even through multiple layers of clothing, he could feel the warmth of her body, tempting on such a cold day. It made him want to pull her even closer into an actual embrace. He clenched his jaw, resolving to ignore that unseemly impulse.

With just a few long strides, he stepped out of the water and onto dry gravel again. He put Miss Burnley down gently and politely looked away while she straightened her red cloak. His whole face felt aflame, and he could only hope that his embarrassment looked less obvious than it felt.

"Thank you, my lord." She sounded as embarrassed as him. They walked in silence for a few minutes before she spoke again. "I hope they find the missing jewels."

"I hope so too." Richard was tired of talking about the stolen jewels, but the subject might stop him from recalling the sensation of having an attractive woman in his arms. Uninvited memories of Miss Burnley's bosom brushing up against his chest kept disturbing his mind. It could not be respectful for him to keep thinking of one of his guests that way. Better to go over the painful topic of the stolen jewels again than to dwell on such images!

"I suppose the guests will talk about nothing but the theft until the jewels are found," he said. And if they were not found? Richard would have to replace them as best he could, though their family history probably made them priceless in their owners' eyes. He sighed as he imagined the apologies he would have to make.

"Is it possible that Lady Canning's jewels were just misplaced?" Miss Burnley suggested.

Richard smiled wryly. "I wish it were possible. I would rather think that someone got careless with them than that we have a thief in our midst. But if they had merely been misplaced, they should have turned up by now."

It did not seem at all likely that so many valuable objects could have been accidentally misplaced in so short a time. But of course, none of the other guests knew about the missing fish forks or Richard's missing stickpin. He had been wrong to conceal the earlier thefts, hadn't he? If he had warned everyone to guard their valuables, the rubies might still be safe.

At this very moment, Gibson and Mrs. Cadwallader were searching every nook and cranny of the castle. But Richard did not feel very optimistic about their chances of finding Lady Canning's jewels, or any of the other missing items. Whoever stole them was probably clever enough to think of a good hiding place. For all he knew, the purloined treasures might be hidden somewhere about the grounds rather than in the castle. Now, *that* was a daunting thought indeed!

He darted a sideways glance at Miss Burnley, relieved to see her looking calm and cheerful, apparently no longer rattled by the puddle incident. Probably only he kept thinking about that.

"You need not worry about the theft, Miss Burnley," he assured her. "Just make sure you keep your valuables well secured."

She laughed and wrinkled her nose. "I haven't many valuables to worry about—only a pearl necklace and a signet ring."

"Oh? A ring with the Burnley family seal?" He was not familiar with the Burnley family or its coat of arms.

She hesitated before answering. "Yes, I suppose so. All I know is that it belonged to my father."

For some reason—he could not have said why—Richard had the impression that she was prevaricating. He could think of no reason why she would lie about a piece of heirloom jewelry. But as he studied her face, he became increasingly convinced that something about the conversation troubled her.

It would be most polite to change the subject, he decided. "Didn't you tell me you had a birthday coming up?"

Her expression lightened at once. "As a matter of fact, it is today."

"Today?" Richard stopped in his tracks, surprised. How could he have forgotten that? He ought to have asked the cook to prepare something special for dinner. Perhaps it was not too late? He pondered that as he resumed walking. At the very least, he should ask Lady Rufford about Miss Burnley's favorite desserts.

"You were born on Christmas Eve, then?" The moment he asked, he recognized how redundant the question was. If today was her birthday, the answer was obviously yes.

But she merely smiled at the question. "Yes. That is why I was named Ivy. My mother wanted to name me 'Holly,' but my Aunt Rufford convinced her that 'Ivy' was a prettier name and just as festive. I believe she took it from the carol 'Green Groweth the Holly.'" She chuckled. "I am fortunate not to have been named Yule Log or Mistletoe!"

Richard laughed too, though he could not imagine any parent so foolish as to name a child "Yule Log." His gaze met Miss

Burnley's, and her smile perceptibly widened. Her whole face was alight with humor. He caught his breath at the sight. Then he told himself he merely felt glad that at least *one* guest was enjoying the house party.

"What did your father think of the name?" he asked.

Her face immediately fell. "I have no memory of him. I don't think anyone knows what he thought about it." She had been looking up at Richard, but now she dropped her gaze to study the path before them.

"I am sorry." Clearly, Richard had touched a sore spot again. "It must have been difficult growing up without knowing your parents."

"Yes. Rather." The short, clipped words suggested she felt strongly about this—and did not want to talk about it.

Richard cast about for something more innocuous to say. "Are you very fond of Christmas?" He knew it was an inane thing to ask, but he wanted to avoid accidentally offending Miss Burnley again. There could be no reason for him to ask personal questions about her family, anyway.

He must have hit on the right topic, because her face relaxed slightly. "It is one of my favorite times of year. Normally, I would be helping decorate the parish church on Christmas Eve."

Too late, he remembered her telling him she was unhappy about spending Christmas away from home. This was a very infelicitous conversation indeed! But he could think of nothing else to talk about. What did people even discuss, anyway? Was the weather the only safe topic between strangers? He did not understand why this conversation seemed so difficult. As a clergyman, he'd had to talk to people from all ranks and walks of life. He was not used to being at a loss for words.

"It still feels strange not to be polishing up my Christmas sermon," he confessed. "I spent so many years working as a clergyman, and Christmas was one of our busiest times of the year. I hardly know what to do with myself now that someone else is managing the parish." Hosting a house party required exertion, too, but it was a very different kind of work. He was not yet used to hospitality on so grand a scale.

"Lord Francis seems to have something other than sermons on his mind at the moment." Miss Burnley jerked her chin in the direction of the trio walking a few yards ahead of them.

"Too true," Richard agreed. Miss Rufford was laughing at something Lord Francis had said, and the young vicar grinned down at her in a surprisingly familiar way, given that the Ruffords had only been at the castle for a week. But then, matches were sometimes made very quickly at parties like these.

With that thought in mind, Richard looked around, wondering what Rowland was doing. Was he perhaps escorting Miss Canning? To his disappointment, he spied his brother deep in conversation with Lord Crowthorne. The two gentlemen lagged at the end of the walking party, entirely ignoring Miss Canning. He sighed. Nothing about this party was going right!

"Is something wrong?" Miss Burnley looked up at him with surprise.

"Nothing," he said hastily. He did not want to discuss his matchmaking scheme with someone outside the family, particularly when it was going so poorly. "I hope tonight we can finally have a game of charades. My brother thinks his team will win, but—"

Miss Burnley laughed. "Brothers always think that." He wondered how she knew that, when she had no siblings. But given how she had reacted to some of his questions, he did not want to ask.

Chapter Six

CHRISTMAS EVE AT Selwyn Castle was very different from Christmas Eve at Rufford Manor, Ivy discovered. At home, Ivy would have begun her birthday with chocolate and biscuits in bed, and she would have spent much of the day curled up in a warm chair with whatever new novel Uncle Rufford had given her. If the weather allowed, she would have ridden with Rose, a groom trailing behind them for safety.

Later in the day, carolers from the village of Underdown would show up to sing "Here We Come A-Wassailing," "I Saw Three Ships Come Sailing In," and "We Wish You a Merry Christmas." Sometimes, for Ivy's sake, they would sing "Green Groweth the Holly." Somehow, everyone knew it was the song for which she had been named. Christmas Eve always ended with Uncle Rufford reading from the Gospel of Luke, with the whole household gathered to listen.

But today she had none of those birthday rituals to comfort her. The carolers from Ingleton had come and gone a few days ago, so there would be no singing today. Uncle Rufford gave her a handsomely bound copy of *The Tale of Old Mortality*, but Ivy had no time to snuggle in an armchair and read, though she liked Sir Walter Scott's novels. As soon as the guests returned from their winter walk, it was time to decorate the house. At Selwyn Castle, tradition called for the family hanging up the greenery themselves, rather than having servants do it. Lady Agatha Selwyn supervised the decoration, and most of the guests helped.

They began by hanging up garlands in the Great Hall. Ivy found herself working alongside Mr. Selwyn, who kept up a series of silly jokes that made it hard to concentrate on the greenery. Mr. Selwyn looked very like his older brother, minus the silvered hair, but his personality seemed quite different.

When they were nearly finished, Mr. Selwyn leaned his head close to Ivy's and whispered conspiratorially: "No one has ever yet caught Richard under the mistletoe, you know. Will you help make this the year that changes?"

"What?" Ivy's eyes widened. "What do you mean?"

"At Selwyn Castle," he explained, "we don't hang the kissing bough in a doorway. My father always said it was not fair play to put it in an entryway, because then people had no choice about whether to pass beneath it. Instead, we hang it in front of the drawing room fire. That makes it easy to avoid if one does not wish to be kissed. *Too* easy."

He shook his head solemnly, though his eyes danced with mischief. "Richard always avoids the kissing bough. I believe he thought it unseemly for a man of the cloth to go about kissing girls indiscriminately. But he is not a clergyman anymore, is he? He has no excuse to ignore such time-honored holiday traditions." He grinned roguishly.

Ivy opened her mouth to protest, but Mr. Selwyn hurried to clarify before she could say anything for or against his scheme. "I am not asking you to do anything shocking, mind. Just a simple kiss on the cheek. I will distract him, and you can sneak up on him."

Ivy could not hold back a gurgle of laughter. "Sneak up on him? What makes you think I have any skill in stalking prey?" The bigger objection, though, was that it really *wasn't* fair play to trap someone like that.

"I am sure you make a charming huntress," he said gallantly. "Will you at least try?"

"Only if he has a sporting chance to escape." Privately, Ivy thought it a very foolish idea. Why should Mr. Selwyn care whether or not his brother got kissed on Christmas Eve?

Before they dressed for dinner, Aunt Rufford surprised Ivy with a second, unlooked-for birthday gift: a tear-drop-shaped emerald pendant on a gold chain. "This is too grand for me!" Ivy exclaimed. She rarely wore jewelry, and when she did, it was simpler than this.

But, she reminded herself, she had just turned five-and-twenty. Perhaps she no longer needed to dress like a young girl. Her surprise faded into admiration and gratitude. "Thank you, Aunt Rufford. I will wear it tonight."

The second birthday surprise appeared at dinner: a bread pudding stuffed with currants and orange peel. Bread pudding was so popular a dessert that its presence on the table could have been a coincidence, but the addition of orange peel was less common. Someone must have told the cook that Ivy particularly liked it that way. Most likely that was Aunt Rufford's doing, too. How thoughtful of her! Ivy ate the pudding slowly, savoring every bite. It felt disloyal to admit, but this tasted better than the recipe used by the cook at Rufford Manor.

When the women withdrew after dinner, leaving the men to their drinks, the happy chatter took on a darker edge. Lady Canning bemoaned the loss of her rubies, and the Marchioness of Reading feared her jewels might be next. Lady Rufford worried about her diamonds, a gift from her late father. The younger women did not have such treasures to worry about, but they speculated about the identity of the thief.

"It must be a servant, of course," Rose declared. "No gentleman would steal from a lady!" A murmur of assent rose from the other women.

"But if it *were* a gentleman," Ivy suggested, "he might be relying on the fact that we would all suspect the servants. It could be a form of . . . of misdirection." She frowned, knowing that wasn't quite the right word. But she could not think of how better to articulate her belief that one of the guests might hope to pin the crime on a servant.

"Surely you don't believe one of the guests could have stolen the jewels?" Rose stared at Ivy, her eyes wide with surprise. "Everyone here is so very charming and kind and . . . and gentlemanly." For some reason, she blushed after she spoke.

That blush caught Ivy's watchful eye, and she studied her cousin thoughtfully. Did Rose have a particular gentleman in mind? Someone she found especially charming? Rose had certainly spent a good deal of time with both Mr. Canning and Lord Francis, so she might have developed a *tendre* for one of them.

If Rose favored one of the guests, she had not admitted as much to Ivy. That bothered Ivy. Her cousin had always looked up to Ivy, who was six years Rose's senior. Last year, when Rose's governess retired, Ivy took on a mentoring role to her young cousin. It surprised her that Rose had not confided her feelings to Ivy—assuming that she had special feelings for one of the gentlemen. But the two cousins had not had as much time to chat alone as they would have had at Rufford Manor. Maybe that was to blame.

Ivy had no opportunity to pry further into the meaning behind Rose's blush, because the gentlemen entered the drawing room, laughing and talking amongst themselves. The women immediately dropped the topic of the missing jewels in favor of other diversions, and the mood in the room lightened.

"I believe we are to play charades tonight, yes?" Mr. Selwyn said jovially. "I choose Miss Rufford for my team." He took a chair near Rose, who smiled shyly at him.

"Always picking the prettiest girls, are you?" Lord Crowthorne drawled. "I believe I will join your team as well." He wandered over to stand by Mr. Selwyn's side.

Everyone else chose sides too, whether by inclination or simple proximity. Ivy found herself on Lord Inglewhite's team, competing against her own cousin. Lord Inglewhite's team was at a distinct disadvantage. His brother had somehow drawn most of the lively, playful members of the party to his side, leaving Lord Inglewhite with a team of people who really did not want to put themselves out too much for the sake of a game.

Ivy did her best, but she had little acting ability, unlike Rose, who pantomimed a falling leaf so gracefully that her team correctly guessed the word was "Autumn." Ivy would have had no idea how to act that out. She was not particularly surprised when Mr. Selwyn's team soundly defeated hers.

"Well, friends, we gave it our all," Lord Inglewhite concluded when the game ended. On the opposite end of the drawing room, Mr. Selwyn (apparently not a graceful winner, at least when playing against his older brother) lead his team in a ridiculous victory cheer. Ivy struggled to keep a straight face, and finally gave up.

"We lack the verve of your brother's team," she suggested once she stopped chuckling. "It is hard to compete against so much spirit."

"I suppose it is." Lord Inglewhite wrinkled his nose ruefully. Then he turned his head in the direction of the double doors. The doors swung open, and the butler carried in a heavy tray bearing a bowl of steaming punch.

Ivy drew a deep, appreciative breath. She could smell the spicy citrus blend from here, and her mouth watered. But before she could get a glass of punch, Rose approached her with a series of questions about the game.

Instead of snagging a hot drink, Ivy found herself trying to explain why she had so much trouble acting out "horsemanship," a word with which she and most of her team were quite familiar. The "horse" part had been easy, since she still remembered a childhood when she spent half her time pretending to be a horse. The second half of the word, however, posed a problem. Her attempt to walk around like a "man" failed so completely that she gave up before trying to act out "ship." It was no wonder her team could not guess the word.

As they talked, Ivy tried to edge towards the punch bowl. She feared all the punch might disappear before she could get a cup. But Rose, who kept shivering and rubbing her arms, wanted to move towards the fire. Ivy followed her cousin patiently, though she hoped the conversation would end soon and leave her free to grab some punch. They ended up standing right in front of the fireplace. It was, she had to admit, a warm and cozy place to chat. It was just so very far from the punchbowl!

"Oh, thank you, Mr. Selwyn!" Rose chirped. "A cup of punch would be most welcome!" Much to Ivy's annoyance, Rose abandoned her right in the middle of a sentence to go accept a drink from that gentleman.

Ivy shook her head at this dereliction. She turned to walk towards the punch bowl herself. But the journey was unnecessary, because Lord Inglewhite stepped in front of her, holding a cup filled near to the brim.

"Miss Burnley, my brother thought you might appreciate a hot drink. Would you care for a glass of punch?"

"Oh, yes!" She took the cup gratefully and took a cautious sip, not wanting to burn her tongue. The punch tasted every bit as good—and as strong—as she had imagined. She blissfully closed her eyes and let the flavor roll across her tongue. She might be far from home, but this part of Christmas tasted exactly as it should.

She had taken only a few careful sips before someone (she suspected Mr. Selwyn) called out: "Look! Inglewhite is standing under the mistletoe!"

She looked up and saw that the mistletoe hung roughly over-head—at least, over *her* head. But Lord Inglewhite was not standing so close as to be considered under the mistletoe with her, in her opinion. Mr. Selwyn's plan had failed.

"I am *not!*" Lord Inglewhite protested. He scowled across the room at his brother. "I am at least two feet away from the mistletoe!"

"That's close enough," Lady Agatha declared. "You must kiss Miss Burnley." She smiled serenely, looking confident that her nephew would do as he was told.

The whole party turned to stare at them, giving Ivy the distinct impression that she and Lord Inglewhite had somehow become the target of a conspiracy.

Lord Inglewhite glared at his younger brother. Then he looked back at Ivy and smiled sheepishly. "I suppose we had better do as they ask, or we will never hear the end of it."

"It *is* a holiday tradition." Ivy meant to speak confidently, as if it did not matter at all, but her voice sounded hushed and breathless, and her heart pounded. Goodness, you would think she had never been kissed under the mistletoe before! Of course, she had never kissed an *earl* before. Probably Lord Inglewhite's high position was all that made her nervous.

Certainly, there could be nothing about Lord Inglewhite's behavior to make a young woman feel uncomfortable around him. He seemed a kind and considerate man, and he had been quite respectful when he lifted her over the puddle this afternoon. But thinking of that moment was a mistake. The memory of his scent—wool and earthy cologne mingled together—was strong enough to distract her even from the rich aroma of the punch in her hand. Recalling his hands on her waist made Ivy's heart race even faster as he lowered his head and pressed his lips lightly against her cheek.

Oh, was that all? Ivy blinked in surprise. She had expected a proper kiss. But of course, Lord Inglewhite only kissed her for the sake of tradition. It was not as if he fancied her! And it was better that he *not* fancy her, all things considered. She could have no cause for disappointment. Ivy forced herself to smile as she stepped back from the earl.

Lord Inglewhite turned and glared at his younger brother again. "There? Does that make you happy, Rowland?"

"No." Mr. Selwyn crossed his arms in front of his chest as he shook his head. "You kissed her, but *she* did not kiss *you*. Miss Burnley, you must kiss Inglewhite now."

"Oh!" A blush burned Ivy's cheeks. All eyes in the room

seemed to point straight at her, eager to see what she would do. She felt like a fox at bay, her heart hammering in her chest.

"Rowland, stop that," Lord Inglewhite said sharply. "You have embarrassed the poor girl enough. Do not force her to do something she dislikes."

Ivy opened her mouth to say that she would not have disliked kissing Lord Inglewhite, but she caught herself in time. She could not say so embarrassing a thing, even though it was true. A lady's partiality for a gentleman ought not be revealed until the gentleman declared his affections first. At least, everyone said so, though the rule had never made much sense to Ivy.

Until this very moment, she had not realized that she wanted to kiss Lord Inglewhite. But she did. She would have liked to discover what the stubble rising on his jawline felt like against her lips. She would have liked to feel his lips pressed against hers. She would have liked . . . She swallowed uneasily as she tried to rein in her unexpectedly unruly thoughts.

Oh, dear. She had conceived a *tendre* for Lord Inglewhite, hadn't she? It had happened before. She had always tried to ignore her feelings, to hide them from the object of her affection, knowing she would not make a suitable wife for a gentleman.

Perhaps if a man from a more modest station of life—say, a gentleman farmer, or a young surgeon or solicitor—had sought her favor, she would have considered marrying him, hoping her background would not disgrace him. For of course, she would have told the truth to any man before accepting him. But men of such modest means rarely approached wealthy young ladies who were the wards of the local baron.

"I think I am done with the mistletoe for the night," she announced. "My apologies for disappointing you, Mr. Selwyn. But I do not feel well." She tried to smile, but her smile felt stiff and unnatural. She hoped that no one could tell how uncomfortable she felt.

Lord Inglewhite leaned toward her and whispered: "I am very sorry my brother's poor taste should so discomfit you. And I am sorry if I contributed to your discomfort."

"You did nothing wrong." She tried to infuse her voice with good humor she did not really feel. "It is merely that I have a headache. If you will excuse me, my lord, I had better go rest."

She hurried out of the room, knowing she was moving too quickly for good manners. But she could not seem to slow herself down to a gentle, dispassionate walk. When she got to the second story, she breathed a little more easily. She let the mask of polite good temper fall from her face, since there was no one here to read her true feelings.

Even so, she did not cry when she reached her room. Instead, she sat down at the chair in front of her dressing table and calmly removed her jewelry. When she put away her new pendant, she checked to make sure her father's signet ring was still there, just in case. Not that the jewel thief would be likely to visit her room, of course. It must be obvious to everyone at the party that she did not wear expensive jewelry.

Yes, she found the ring right where it should be, looking as it always did. The seal was made of a dark stone threaded with white, carved with an intaglio design of a winged lion crouched over a book. The vicar of St. Sebastian's had told her that the winged lion was a symbol associated with St. Mark, the evangelist. But he did not know whose coat of arms it was. Nor did Lord Rufford recognize it.

Ivy supposed she could have consulted a book on heraldry, or found an expert on the subject. Someone, somewhere, must know whose family the ring belonged to. But she had never tried very hard to find out. She did not know want to know the true identity of the man who had seduced and abandoned her mother. She did not want to have any kind of relationship with such a man, whoever he might be. Her mother had chosen not to seek him out once she realized he had abandoned her, and Ivy had always felt she owed it to her mother to respect that wish.

Besides, learning her father's true identity could not alter the shame of Ivy's illegitimacy. A child born out of wedlock could never be legitimated. She would always bear the stigma of her birth. Therefore, she would never sully the name of a gentleman—worse yet, a *nobleman*—by forming an alliance with a respectable house. No matter how attractive that nobleman might be.

So, she must put aside her preference for the Earl of Inglewhite. Even if he returned her feelings (which he clearly did not), she could never marry him. She did not want to burden so good a man with the disgrace of her birth. It was a shame, though. She had known him only a week, but she had seen enough to suspect he would make an excellent husband. But he could never be *her* husband. That would not be right.

And she would not cry about it. Some hurts ran too deep for tears.

Chapter Seven

AFTER MOST OF the guests had gone to bed, Richard lingered in the library, reading a few letters that could not be ignored. One of them demanded an immediate answer, so he pulled out his stationery and began to write. Hopefully, this mundane chore would help him put all the vicissitudes of the day out of his mind so he could rest rather than staying up all night fretting over his mistakes.

"I thought I would find you here." Rowland stood in the doorway, leaning casually against the door frame. He shook his head. The set of his mouth looked stern, but his laughing eyes contradicted it. "It is so very like you to be working late on Christmas Eve. Richard, do you never take a holiday?"

"I am on holiday right now!" Richard grumbled. "In case you have not noticed, I am hosting a Christmas party. You must have had too much punch."

"You have not nearly had enough punch," Rowland scolded. "I handed you the perfect opportunity to flirt with Miss Burnley, and you wasted it! I would say you did not know how to woo a woman, except that you have done it successfully before, and—"

"What on earth are you prattling about now?" Richard demanded. "I am not trying to woo anyone. I have had enough of courtship. You ought to know that!"

Rowland stared, his mouth falling open a fraction. "What

nonsense are *you* going on about?"

"I tried to marry." Richard stared down at the half-written letter on his desk, avoiding his brother's eyes. "I tried twice. Neither time did it work out. At my time of life, it would be ludicrous to try again. I have no intention of courting anyone." No further courtships meant no more heartache.

"What happened to Amabel was tragic." All traces of amusement left Rowland's eyes, and his voice gentled. "I can only guess at how much it hurt. But that was years ago, Richard. Surely you have had time to grieve your fiancée's death? And you must marry. You need an heir."

"I do not need an heir when I have a younger brother in good health," Richard snapped. "A brother who is the perfect age for matrimony." Rowland could not be this oblivious! He must have understood the purpose of this party.

Rowland's eyes widened. "Dear God, you don't mean you invited all these young ladies here for me? I thought they were for you!" He sounded genuinely shocked.

Richard stared back at his brother. He probably looked as confused as Rowland. He certainly felt shaken. "You thought I invited marriageable young ladies so I could choose a countess? But that is ridiculous! In case you have not noticed, I am a middle-aged man now. I ought not marry a girl just out of the schoolroom. And I wouldn't want to do so!"

"I was a little surprised that you invited Miss Rufford," Rowland acknowledged. "She seems much too young. Rather childish, in fact. But I thought, perhaps"—he glanced away, as if embarrassed—"you wanted a young bride. One with many childbearing years ahead of her."

"I don't want any bride!" Richard cringed at the rising volume of his voice. He must do better at controlling his temper. His brother deserved better than to be yelled at as if he were a naughty child. "I invited Miss Rufford here because I hoped she might take *your* fancy." He glared at Rowland. "I thought that was obvious." Lord Rufford's only daughter would have made a perfectly acceptable bride for Rowland.

"My God." Rowland shook his head again. He walked to the nearest armchair and abruptly dropped into it, as if his legs felt weak. "You really don't know, do you?"

"Know what?" Richard cocked his head to one side, puzzled. "I know you've enjoyed being a carefree man about town, but I thought we were in agreement that you ought to settle down and marry. Didn't we talk about that?"

Rowland's shoulders slumped and he stared down at the floor. "We talked about me settling down and putting an end to my rackety ways, yes," he agreed. "You are right about me getting too old to stay up all night gambling and . . . and sporting. But we never spoke of marriage. If I had known you had this in mind, I would have. . . ." He fell silent, not completing the thought.

"You would have what?" Richard stared at his brother. He had no idea where this conversation was going.

"I would have told you the truth." Rowland sighed. "I thought perhaps you had guessed. But I suppose I should have known better. You always were so unworldly. It would never even occur to you, would it?"

"What would never occur to me?" The more Rowland said, the more mystified Richard felt. "What truth about you do I not know?" Richard knew everything about his younger brother, didn't he? What foods he liked, what things he feared, what games were his favorite. Though they were seven years apart in age, they had always been attached to each other. All three of the Selwyn brothers had been on friendly terms, at least once they grew out of the most quarrelsome stage of boyhood.

Rowland sighed and ran a hand across his face, tousling his fashionably styled hair. "You were a clergyman once, so you must know a good deal about human weakness. But you are also my brother, and I don't want to burden you with the knowledge of my sins. Suffice it to say, Richard, that I will never marry, because I do not desire women the way a husband should desire his wife."

"What do you mean?" Richard's mind raced as he tried to make sense of his brother's words. "You don't mean. . ." He let his voice trail off as all the possible implications sank in.

Rowland didn't mean to say that he desired men, did he? Surely Richard would have known if that were the case! He ransacked his memory, looking for any signs of such a preference. He could think of no positive evidence to support the theory. But then, he could think of no evidence against it, either.

True, Rowland had always been the life of the party, flirting indiscriminately with any woman willing to flirt back. But he had never once talked of having a *tendre* for any woman, not even in his boyhood. His name had never been linked with any of the widows or married women in London society who were known to take lovers. So far as Richard knew, Rowland had never kept a mistress. And he had certainly never attempted anything even remotely like a serious courtship of an eligible young lady. Richard had assumed this was because his brother was not yet ready to settle down. Now he considered an alternative explanation.

Rowland looked steadily away from him. "I do not desire women," he repeated. "Let us leave it at that. You do not need to know more than that. But you must understand that I mean it when I say you cannot expect an heir from *me*."

"I see." Richard sat in stunned silence until he could bring himself to speak. "Well. I suppose it is good that you told me that before I tried any harder to arrange a match for you."

Rowland snorted derisively. "Precisely."

Richard gazed into the smoldering remnants of the fire, trying to master his tumultuous emotions. As a clergyman, he was horrified by the possibility that Rowland might have committed so egregious a sin as his words implied. Lust was a common enough sin, true, but *this* form of lust? Richard had always been told it was unnatural. There must be a reason why sodomy was punishable by the death penalty, mustn't there?

But, on the other hand, this was his beloved baby brother,

who even as a child had always been a stickler for fair play and good sportsmanship. Who, whatever his faults, had always been kind and generous. Richard did not believe Rowland was capable of grave wrongdoing. If he had violated both law and commonly accepted morals, he must have had good reason to do so.

Rowland might gamble away more of his income than he ought to, and he might neglect his career, but he would never do anything *evil*. Richard felt confident of that. Therefore, it logically followed that whatever Rowland might or might not have done could not be truly evil. As he slowly and silently thought through the matter, Richard began to regain his composure.

Even so, he waited until he worked out the right words before he broke the silence. "Thank you for your confidence. I think you are right not to tell me any more of the details. Especially if they might incriminate anyone else."

It was one thing for Rowland to admit to his own proclivities, but given the legal issues at stake, it would be inappropriate for the brothers to discuss the actions of any other people who might have been involved. Even though Richard now found himself wondering if any of the male friends Rowland had brought home during school and university vacations had, in fact, been more than friends.

His initial dismay at Rowland's revelation faded, only to be replaced by more complicated emotions. He silently confronted the fact that there was a side of his brother's life he might never know about. There might be people Rowland loved whom Richard could never publicly accept as part of the family. People whom Richard might never even meet! That broke his heart.

"I will, of course, never reveal this information to anyone else," Richard promised. He cleared his throat, still gazing into the fire rather than looking into his brother's eyes. "And I want you to know that I trust your, ah, judgment and moral character. If your heart does not condemn any of your actions, then neither do I."

"Thank you for that," Rowland replied. They sat together in

silence for a long time, listening to the occasional pop from the dying fire.

Again, Richard broke the silence. "But who is going to inherit Selwyn Castle after I die, then?" They did not have any male first cousins in the line of succession. He would have to dig up the family tree to see who was next in line.

"I had assumed your son would inherit after you." Rowland sounded as if he were trying not to laugh. "Since I know perfectly well that *you* find women attractive. I mean, I may not have always agreed with your taste—the former Miss Dixon being a case in point—but you were rather young then, and I am sure you will make a better choice now that you are older and wiser. There was nothing in the least wrong with Amabel, after all. She was an excellent choice."

The amusement in Rowland's voice grated on Richard's ears. "Oh, do stop laughing at me," he grumbled. "It is not in the least bit funny! I am too old to get married."

Rowland abandoned any attempt to contain his amusement and laughed heartily. "Too old at seven-and-thirty? Really? Balderdash! You mean you are too stubborn and set in your ways. Richard, I know you have had to make many adjustments in your life after Robert's death . . ." The laughter faded from his voice as he mentioned their too-recent loss. Then he cleared his throat. "I think you should consider matrimony as merely one of the necessary changes that come with inheriting the title."

Easy for him to say when he was not the one forced to seek a bride! "And how, exactly, do you think I am supposed to find a wife at this time of my life? Who do you imagine is going to want to marry me?" Richard demanded.

Rowland started chuckling again. When Richard glared at him, he manfully controlled his expression, though the laughter still shone out of his eyes. "I should think a great many women would like to be a countess. And I suspect many of them would not have the least objection to your supposed old age. But you are going to have to ask them, not me." Rowland looked away quickly, but this time Richard suspected he did so because he was trying to restrain his laughter.

Richard buried his face in his hands for a moment, overwhelmed by the magnitude of the task before him. Then he lifted his head and announced: "This is ridiculous! I invited all these guests with *you* in mind, not me. None of the young ladies here are the least bit suitable."

"Not the younger ones, no," Rowland agreed. "But why do you think I tried to get Miss Burnley under the mistletoe with you? She seems a sensible young woman, and she is a full five-and-twenty. I thought she might suit you better than some child still in her teens. *And* I saw the two of you getting along quite well during today's walk." He lifted his eyebrows suggestively.

"I never asked you to matchmake for me!" Richard's face burned. He had not realized that Rowland noticed the puddle incident.

"I never asked *you* to matchmake for *me*," Rowland reminded him. "And yet, that was the apparent purpose of this party. Now I finally understand why you were so insistent that I come home instead of staying in London for the winter!" His shoulders started shaking with laughter again.

This time, Richard joined him. He had finally seen the humor in the fact that, while Richard had been fruitlessly attempting to find a wife for his younger brother, Rowland had been trying to arrange a match for *him*. Apparently, they still thought alike.

"Yes, yes, it's very amusing," Richard said once he could stop laughing. "All the same, even if I had a preference for Miss Burnley—which I am not admitting to be the case, mind you—I see no indication that she has any such preference for me."

His face fell as he remembered the way Miss Burnley had practically run out of the room to avoid kissing him. If anything, that seemed like a sign of aversion. Had he offended her during that encounter under the mistletoe? After his experience during the afternoon walk, he tried to restrain his unexpectedly libidinous desires in favor of a chaste kiss on the cheek, but perhaps he would have done better to decline to kiss her at all.

Rowland nodded. "Yes, I know. You are going to have to try harder to win her, old chap."

"I wasn't trying at all!" Richard said indignantly, and the two of them collapsed into laughter again. Later, Richard knew, he would have to think the matter through more seriously. Rowland was probably right that Miss Burnley would suit him better than the other marriageable women at the party. Richard could not deny that she attracted him. But after their disastrous encounter under the mistletoe, he feared the attraction might be one-sided.

For now, he set all those concerns aside in order to share a moment of mirth with his brother. Perhaps, after all, their hilarity was less a true expression of humor and more a side-effect of the tensions at play in this night's very personal conversation. Maybe the brothers laughed with relief at having cleared the air. But either way, it felt good to laugh together, even if Richard himself was the butt of the joke.

Chapter Eight

CHRISTMAS MORNING DAWNED crisp and cold. Gray clouds covered the sky. When Ivy first stepped outside on her way to church, she drew a deep breath. Was that snow she smelled? A hopeful smile lit up her face. Maybe it would be a white Christmas. That did not seem to happen as often in real life as it did in holiday prints, but one could hope.

St. John's church was a small but well-kept building, boasting beautiful stained glass windows. A vicarage flanked it on one side and a churchyard on the other. Ivy spared a glance at the latter as she alighted from the carriage. Her eye was immediately drawn to a large mausoleum. Probably the Selwyn dead rested there.

Perhaps she would have a chance to walk among the gravestones, hopefully on a warmer day. Ivy liked to read the epitaphs and to study the names of previous generations. She was fascinated by the way "John" and "Mary" stayed in style for centuries, while names like "Hezekiah" or "Chloris" came and went. She rarely found her own name on grave markers, so when she did stumble across another "Ivy," it was a pleasant surprise.

Not everyone from the house party wished to attend Christmas services, but there were still too many people for the Inglewhite pew, so the party spilled over into an unused pew. Ivy did not even look to see if there was room for her in the Inglewhite pew. She led Rose into the adjacent pew, which had a view nearly as good. Young Mr. Canning followed them and, probably to no one's surprise, sat next to Rose.

But Lord Inglewhite surprised Ivy by taking the seat beside her. "You are not sitting in your own pew?" she asked. "Why not?"

He rolled his eyes. "My younger brother took the place where I usually sit, and rather than fight him for it, I came here. The family who uses this pew is in Yorkshire right now, so they will not mind us sitting here."

Not a very convincing explanation, in Ivy's opinion. Wouldn't it have made more sense for him to choose a different seat in his own pew? It seemed strange for the Earl of Inglewhite to sit anywhere but in the Inglewhite family pew. Indeed, other parishioners looked at him with surprise. But maybe she imagined that.

"Does it feel strange to be a member of the congregation in the church that used to be yours?" she asked him.

He smiled. "Very strange. Lord Francis is an excellent cleric, but sometimes I have to force myself not to fault him for doing things differently than I would have done. His sermons are always shorter than mine were, for instance, and he quotes from Patristic authors rather than Jeremy Taylor or William Law."

"Patristic authors?" she repeated doubtfully. She supposed that was better than citing Baxter or Whitefield.

"People like Augustine of Hippo," he clarified, "and John Chrysostom."

Ivy intended to say something about *Confessions*, that being the only work of Augustine's she had read, but then the service began, and the time for conversation ended.

The best part of any Christmas service was getting to sing Christmas hymns, beginning with "While Shepherds Watched their Flocks by Night." Ivy did not have as good a singing voice as Rose did, her range being too limited for many songs, but she had a decent sense of pitch and could carry a tune. She loved to sing, whether or not she was good at it.

Lord Francis proved to be a good preacher. Ivy could not imagine anyone having complaints about his Christmas sermon. But perhaps Lord Inglewhite was more critical, having been a vicar himself.

After the service, the castle guests restored themselves with a light luncheon, followed by parlor games, naps, and walks, until it was time for Christmas dinner. Lord Francis had been invited to dine at the castle again, and by now it surprised no one that he escorted Rose into the dining room, leaving Mr. Canning to accompany Ivy.

This time, Ivy ended up with Lord Crowthorne as her other dinner partner. He was polite, but not particularly communicative, and she spent a good part of the meal eating silently. To be sure, she had Mr. Canning by her side, too, but by now she had run out of things to say to him. All she could think of were inane comments about the weather and the jolliness of the holidays. How many times could one person say, "The weather is very seasonable for Christmas?" before they died of despair? She tried to maintain a cheerful chatter, but her heart wasn't in it.

Maybe her dining companions were not the problem. Perhaps she felt dull because of the companion she did *not* have by her side. Ivy suspected she was pining for Lord Inglewhite. But he could not have sat beside her even if he wanted to, since custom required that the most high-ranking women sit next to the host. And what made her think he *wanted* to be near her? He had certainly given no sign of such an inclination!

As dinner progressed, Ivy began to wish she could go home early. Could she manufacture some excuse for returning to Rufford Manor? Perhaps the Ladies' Aide Society might need her help with winter charities? But she did not think her aunt and uncle would be happy about her traveling home by herself. Not even if she took a maid with her. And she could not take a maid, anyway, because she and Rose shared a lady's maid. Rose would need Watts's assistance for the duration of the house party.

Ivy sighed and looked down at the plum pudding before her.

It was drenched with brandy and smelled delicious, but she had no appetite for it.

"Is something wrong, Miss Burnley?" Mr. Canning asked.

"I am merely tired," she explained. "Perhaps I will retire early tonight." She had no more inclination for parlor games or ghost stories than she did for the rich pudding before her. She had grown weary of the whole party.

She lingered with the women after dinner, but when the gentlemen came in after their drinks, she slipped out of the drawing room, intent on going to her room.

When she met Mr. Selwyn in the corridor, he greeted her with dismay. "Miss Burnley, you're not leaving already? The party is just getting started!"

Ivy repeated her excuse: "I am very tired tonight." She might have gotten away, had not Lord Inglewhite followed his brother.

His lordship smiled at her. "Miss Burnley, do you know any good ghost stories? We did not tell stories last night, so we ought to do it tonight."

"I know a few," she began, "but—"

"Excellent!" young Mr. Selwyn said. "You will have to share them with us. We are tired of hearing the same stories every year."

The younger Selwyn brother took her by the arm, and before Ivy could further protest, he steered her back into the drawing room. She found herself placed in a comfortable chair by the fire—a chair she felt certain had been reserved for Lord Inglewhite. Now there was no escape.

Ivy *did* like ghost stories, though she was not particularly good at telling them. She contributed to the night's entertainment by relating a legend about a child ghost who haunted the nursery of an estate not far from Bristol. She had learned the tale from her mother, though she could not reveal her source. After all, her parents were supposed to have died when she was an infant.

After she finished her story, she happily sat back and listened. Mr. Selwyn told a couple of gruesome tales. So did Lord

Crowthorne, who had very good delivery. But, to her surprise, quiet Miss Canning displayed a turn for narrative that outdid all the other storytellers. The story she told was simple and traditional, involving a dying curse, a lady in white, and a family secret. But she delivered it so well, the hairs on the back of Ivy's neck stood on end at the story's climax.

Just when Ivy thought the evening's entertainments had come to an end, Lord Inglewhite spoke. "You know, Selwyn Castle is said to be haunted," he announced.

Someone gasped. Rose squealed theatrically and exchanged a happy look with Miss Canning. The two of them spent a good deal of time together, perhaps because Joshua Canning was trying to fix his interest with Rose.

"Oh, don't tell us about it! You will scare us all and we will not be able to sleep!" Lady Canning protested. But she leaned forward in her chair, as if eager to hear.

"Oh, but *I* want to hear," Lord Francis said. "Now that I live in Ingleton, I ought to know all the local lore." He reached out to pat Rose's hand comfortingly.

Then, Ivy saw, he casually left his hand over hers. Rather forward of him, since they were not betrothed. Ivy chewed on her lower lip thoughtfully and glanced at Lady Rufford, curious whether her aunt had observed the gesture.

Her aunt did indeed have her eyes on Rose, but the corners of her lips curled up in a smile. Apparently, she approved. Lord Francis might be only a younger son, but he already had his own living, so he could probably afford to marry. Rose's sizeable dowry would no doubt add to their comfort.

Ivy was so distracted by the courtship playing out before her eyes that she missed the beginning of the Selwyn Castle ghost story. It involved a ghostly dog of the sort often said to haunt churchyards or highways. The dog lurked on the grounds, and sightings of it supposedly presaged trouble in the family. Ivy wondered idly whether the dog had been seen before the illness that carried away the previous Earl of Inglewhite. But of course,

Lord Inglewhite did not say anything about that. The tragedy with which the story ended had happened generations ago—if, indeed, it ever occurred at all.

No one else volunteered a story after that, perhaps because it seemed fitting to end the storytelling session with a home-grown tale. Some of the ladies started talking about retiring for the night, though no one had yet gotten out of their seats.

Then Sir Michael Canning electrified the whole room with an announcement. "Did you all realize it's been snowing for the last half hour?"

"Snow on Christmas! Perfect!" An eager grin split Mr. Selwyn's face. "Let's go outside and watch the snow fall."

His suggestion was greeted with general approbation, despite the late hour. Lady Agatha declined to venture outside, pleading a weakness to colds, but everyone else wanted to watch the snow fall on Christmas. This was Ivy's chance to sneak away, if she wanted. But she had been hoping for a white Christmas, and she would hate to miss it now. Instead of going up to her room, she followed the rest of the party onto the grassy lawn in front of the house.

One of the footmen fetched a couple of lanterns, giving them light to see despite the overcast night. The snow fell in thick, fluffy clumps. The day had grown colder rather than warmer, and the snow was beginning to stick. There might very well be a layer of white for the Feast of St. Stephen. *Lovely!* Ivy's heart lifted as she watched the snow for a few chilly minutes. Some of her anxieties and unhappiness faded away in the face of such natural beauty.

Then she turned back, thinking it high time she went to bed. The snow was beautiful, and she was glad she had stayed up to see it, but it had been a long day. Besides, she was tired of watching other people flirt.

Lord Inglewhite stood in the doorway, observing his guests. Someone had hung a lantern near the door, and by its light Ivy could see a smile on the nobleman's face. She saw something else, too. A small sprig of mistletoe hung in the middle of the wide doorway, positioned so two people who passed through the doorway at the same time would be caught underneath it. Did Lord Inglewhite know he stood under the mistletoe? Doubtful. All the same, Ivy hesitated before crossing the threshold.

"Merry Christmas, Miss Burnley. I hope you had a pleasant holiday, even though you were away from home." It might have been her imagination, but she thought Lord Inglewhite's smile deepened as he looked into her eyes.

"I did, thank you." She did her best to keep her voice pleasant and her face happy. She had no desire to reveal any of her heartache. But she flicked her eyes up to the mistletoe one last time before stepping forward.

He glanced up, too, and his smile fell. "Who put that there?" he grumbled. "We had enough kissing yesterday."

Did we? Ivy wondered. It had not seemed enough to her, because she had not gotten to kiss Lord Inglewhite. After tonight, the mistletoe would be put away, and she would have lost her chance. Such an opportunity was unlikely to ever present itself again, for there could be no reason for her to return to Selwyn Castle for another Christmas. Once Rose was married, Ivy would not need to attend matchmaking events as her chaperone.

Now or never, then. Ivy made her decision in the span of a racing heartbeat, and did not give herself a chance to second-guess her actions. She stepped closer to the earl, stood on her tiptoes, and kissed him on the cheek. At least, that was what she meant to do. But at the last second, he turned his head a little, and her kiss landed squarely on his mouth. *Oops.*

Startled by this turn of events, Ivy wobbled on her toes. She might have fallen, had Lord Inglewhite not caught her. He steadied her with one hand on either side of her waist. She started to thank him, but she never got the words out, because he lowered his head and kissed her back. Not a quick, friendly kiss, such as anyone might exchange under the kissing bough on Christmas day, but a soft, lingering one of the sort only lovers shared.

For a moment, she let herself savor the feeling of his mouth against hers, his lips teasing at hers. She pressed her mouth against his, hungry for the warmth of his touch. She had not been kissed like this before, but she would not have minded being kissed this way again—or rather, she would not have minded if the situation were different. Her heart ached as she considered all the possible consequences of this exchange. She reluctantly pulled her mouth away from his, wishing she'd had the wisdom to ignore the mistletoe entirely.

What had she done? Lord Inglewhite had misunderstood. Or rather, he understood perfectly well that she fancied him, but did not realize she had no intention of acting on her desire. How could he have known that? And how could Ivy possibly explain his error? Ivy stepped away from him, her heart racing with panic now rather than desire. He immediately let go of her, but he did not break eye contact.

"My Lord," she babbled, "I did not mean . . . it was just the mistletoe, you know. I did not mean anything by it." She swallowed nervously. She had no idea how to say what she needed to say without offending him—or worse, disappointing him. She did not want to hurt him. There was no reason to break his heart as well as her own.

"I am sorry if I misunderstood. And I apologize for my forwardness. But just so we are clear, I *did* mean something by it. I do not play games with women." He spoke softly, but he kept his gaze intently locked with hers.

Her heart thumped erratically in her chest. "Oh. I see." This was the time to indicate she was not interested. She ought to say something to discourage him. But she seemed to have lost the capacity for forming complicated sentences. At the very least, it would have been difficult to deliver a lengthy explanation of her intentions over the lump forming in her throat.

Instead of gently discouraging his suit, she took the cowardly way out. "Merry Christmas, my lord," she whispered. She lowered her eyes as she hurried into the house, not wanting to know what expression he wore. Her heart pounded heavily as she climbed the stairs to her guest room.

When she reached the guestroom corridor, she heard a door closing with a soft click. She flinched, not having expected to find anyone else up here yet. Weren't all the other guests still outside, watching the snowfall? She must not have been the only one to turn in early. No matter. She had nothing to hide but her racing heartbeat.

It was a relief to shut the door to her guestroom behind her. Thank goodness she had a room of her own at this house party! If Rose were sharing her room, she might have noticed something strange about Ivy's behavior. Ivy assumed she must look strange, because she certainly *felt* peculiar.

Over and over again, she heard him saying: "I *did* mean something by it." She could not possibly have misinterpreted those words. The Earl of Inglewhite had taken an interest in Ivy, of all people. But she was no more fit to be the Countess of Inglewhite than to be the Queen of England. What on earth was she going to *do*?

Chapter Nine

OVER AND OVER again, Richard heard her words in his head: "It was just the mistletoe." *Just the mistletoe. It meant nothing.* But Richard remained skeptical. The mistletoe explained why Miss Burnley had kissed him in the first place, yes. She might have meant nothing more than a formal salute to honor the old holiday tradition.

But the presence of mistletoe did not explain why, when he kissed her a second time, she kissed him back so enthusiastically. This was not the first time Richard had kissed a woman. He could tell the difference between a kiss that was merely tolerated and one that was actively shared. Perhaps he fooled himself, but he thought Miss Burnley had enjoyed their kiss as much as he had.

Which left him very uncertain about how to proceed. He liked Miss Burnley, and he would certainly have enjoyed kissing her again, but he had no wish to pursue a reluctant quarry. Maybe Miss Burnley thought him too old to make a good husband. Or perhaps she had not enjoyed their conversations together as much as he had. Or—well, there could be any number of reasons why she might not wish to encourage his suit. He ought to respect her wishes.

There was, strictly speaking, no reason why Richard *had* to choose a bride at this house party. He could find one when he came to London for the Parliamentary session. The Season would provide ample opportunities to meet eligible young ladies. Probably Rowland was right that some of them would overlook Richard's age on account of his title.

But Richard had never been one to shirk a duty. He had an obligation to marry so he could produce the next generation of Selwyns. Given his age, he ought not tarry at that task. He probably owed it to the family to marry the first suitable girl who caught his fancy. Having been raised in a baron's household, Miss Burnley was suitable, and he had to admit she had caught his fancy. Why not marry her? Simply logical!

Even so, he stayed up late into the night, worrying, fretting, and reviewing every interaction he'd had with Miss Burnley since the day she arrived at the castle. He could not tell what she thought about him, and he now regretted that second kiss. She had clearly not expected it, and the way she scurried into the house afterward made him worry that perhaps she had not welcomed it as much as he initially thought.

In truth, he ought not have kissed Miss Burnley at all. Not only were they not engaged, he had not even begun properly courting her. He would never have done it if she had not kissed him first. He had taken that as a sign of interest on her part. Surely proper young ladies did not go around kissing gentlemen whom they did not want to marry?

Then again, Barbara Dixon had kissed him enthusiastically once upon a time, yet she still turned him down when he formally proposed. He sighed, remembering that painful half-hour in the rose garden ten years ago. He had been fervently in love and certain that the object of his affection returned his regard. Her tearful rejection had shaken him to his core. After that, he spent years devoting himself to his career and ignoring the eligible young ladies of his social set, until Amabel Henderson caught his eye.

Richard could have been very happy with Amabel. He fell in love with her slowly, over the better part of a year, and by the end he was far more attached to her than he had ever been to

Barbara Dixon. She loved him deeply in return. For the few precious weeks of their betrothal, their future together looked as rosy as the dawn.

Amabel would have made a fine wife for a young vicar, and she would have done an excellent job as a countess, too. She had been fond of children. If they had married as planned, Richard would probably have had an heir by now. But it seemed that Providence had other plans.

Richard knew he ought not be superstitious, but he could not help wondering if some curse or fate doomed all his courtships to end in disaster. If he were honest with himself, that might have been the real reason he decided to remain a bachelor. His dread of yet another romantic disaster had prompted him to try matchmaking for Rowland rather than for himself. He sighed, thinking of how wrong he had been about *that* scheme.

Now it was all up to Richard to carry on the family legacy. If his third courtship failed, he did not know what he would do. Well, there was always Almack's, he supposed. He had not been there since he was a very young man, but he doubted it had changed much. There would be no shortage of young women on the catch for a husband at London's "Marriage Mart."

He fell asleep still thinking of Almack's, and that night he dreamed of waltzes and quadrilles, lemonade and old-fashioned breeches. To some people it might have been a pleasant dream, but to Richard, it felt more like a nightmare.

The nightmare did not end upon waking, because his valet woke him with the news that someone had stolen Lady Reading's emeralds and Lady Rufford's diamonds. Two thefts in one night! The guests could talk of nothing else at breakfast.

"Enough is enough," Richard announced. "I will send for a Bow Street Runner." He ought to have done so long before now.

He sat down in the study and wrote a letter at once. Then he hurried to smooth down the feelings of the guests as best he could, assuring the ladies that the jewels would be found. He was not surprised when they remained unconvinced. He could not even convince himself.

Apart from sending for a Runner, Richard had no idea what he could do to find the jewels or their thief. Gibson and Mrs. Cadwallader had already searched the castle from top to bottom, and the head gardener and the head groom had searched the outbuildings. No one had found anything in the least bit suspicious, though some missing spades and rakes had shown up in a seldom-used garden shed. The gardener, Weatherstaff, was delighted. He had been looking for them since last spring.

But no one found any jewels or any other contraband. Well, except for the brandy keg in the cellar, which no one claimed to know anything about. Gibson insisted that *he* never purchased smuggled brandy, so Richard could only assume Robert had bought it before his death. Richard did not care for hard liqueur, except as an ingredient in punch, so he let Rowland take possession of the ill-gotten brandy.

After sending the message off to London, Richard walked into the morning room in time to overhear Lady Reading announcing, "This is the worst house party I have ever attended!" She hushed immediately when her eyes fell on Richard, but the damage was done.

He did not blame her. It was the worst house party *he* had ever attended, too. "My lady, I will make this right," he promised. "Somehow." He had no idea how he could afford to replace so much costly jewelry. He could only pray the Bow Street Runner would be able to catch the thief.

The next few days were quiet ones. Richard, knowing he had only two weeks left in which to court Miss Burnley, sought her out as often as he could. The formal seating arrangements prevented him from sitting next to her at dinner, but breakfast was a much less formal meal, with guests coming and going as they liked. Richard asked a few surreptitious questions about Miss Burnley's habits, learning that she typically came down to breakfast only at the very end of the meal, much later than he did.

The next day, therefore, he forced himself to wait nearly an hour longer than usual, despite his grumbling stomach, so that he could sit next to Miss Burnley while she sipped her morning coffee. Richard normally drank tea, but on a whim, he decided to imitate Miss Burnley in drinking coffee. This was a mistake, as he quickly discovered. He had forgotten just how bitter a strong cup of coffee tasted. He hastened to add cream and sugar.

"You must like your coffee sweet, my lord."

Intent on making his drink palatable, Richard flinched when Miss Burnley unexpectedly broke the silence. Cream splashed onto the table. Michael, the footman attending at breakfast, glided from his place to wipe up the spill, but that did not stop Richard from flushing with embarrassment.

"I suppose I do have a sweet tooth," he admitted. He took a sip of his coffee and found, to his dismay, that it was now too sweet even for his tastes. What would happen if he "accidentally" spilled all of it and poured a cup of tea instead? But he could not do that. It would make extra work for young Michael. He gulped his too-sweet drink and tried not to shudder. "Do you like sweets, Miss Burnley?"

"Not in the morning." She took a sip of her coffee and looked down at the newspaper on the table.

That gesture, combined with her indifferent tone, told Richard that his plan had failed. Apparently, Miss Burnley did not care for conversation in the morning. He would have to try to woo her some other way, at some other time of day.

For the rest of the week, he sought out Miss Burnley's company whenever he could. If she read a book in the evening rather than playing cards, he carried the agricultural treatise he was currently struggling with and sat near her so that they could read in silence together. The first time he tried this, he hoped that some opening for conversation might arise. But as the minutes ticked by, he gradually realized that Miss Burnley must be the sort of reader who did not like to be interrupted. Foiled again!

None of these rejections seemed personal, though, so Richard persisted. If nothing else, this at least gave him the chance to learn what books she liked to read and what breakfast foods she liked. That was something, wasn't it? So he told himself, but that did not really assuage either his anxiety or his disappointment over how slowly his courtship progressed—if it could even be said to be progressing at all. .

At least the dry weather allowed for outdoor activities. The guests all seemed happier when they were not confined to the house. On the last day of the year, Richard finally had his chance to show Miss Burnley the path along the banks of the river. He'd wanted to show her this trail since her arrival, but somehow, they had never ridden this way.

But it was not a very successful outing, in Richard's opinion. The chilly wind nipped through his coat despite the thickness of the wool. The path looked particularly uninviting today, too. The snow had long since melted, leaving everything muddy and brown. The trees were brown, the sky was gray, and even the river looked sullen. They might have done better to stay inside by the fire.

Worse, Miss Burnley seemed far more reserved than she had in the past. She responded to Richard's remarks politely but not at all encouragingly. She repeatedly averted her eyes, meeting his gaze only briefly. She did not smile at his mild attempts at wit. And she volunteered nothing about herself. In short, she made it clear that whatever she might have previously done, she did not welcome his attentions today.

It looked like it would have to be Almack's after all. Richard's shoulders slumped with despair at that prospect. It really was a shame. He had thought that he and Miss Burnley might deal well together. It seemed she did not agree.

"Miss Burnley," Richard said at last, "I am very sorry if I have offended you."

She finally glanced up and met his eyes. "You have nothing to apologize for, my lord. You have done no wrong." She shifted her gaze to study the trail before them before speaking further. "I am very sorry if I misled you as to my own intentions."

"You have nothing for which to apologize either," Richard assured her. Though he could not help wondering about the kiss on Christmas Day. Why had she kissed him, if she had not intended to encourage him? She must have spoken the truth when she said she meant nothing by it.

He stared ahead at the trail, confronting the truth: his feeble attempt at a courtship had already failed. This, he thought savagely, was precisely why he had resolved never to marry! He was simply no good at this sort of thing.

If only he had a close male cousin he could train as his heir. Better yet, if only Robert had left a son behind! Then Richard would still be happily managing his parish and trying to settle quarrels among the vestry members. At worst, he might have served as guardian over the estate while the heir grew up. But the Inglewhite title descended to heirs male, so Robert's daughters could not inherit.

"Do you think you will catch the jewel thief?"

Miss Burnley's question, coming out of nowhere, both startled Richard and brought him back down to earth. "I hope so." He glanced over his shoulder to make sure they were still out of earshot of the nearest riders. Then he confessed the truth. "But I have no real confidence about it. I may very well have to reimburse the guests for the missing jewels."

"Lady Reading said her jewels are insured with Lloyd's of London," Miss Burnley replied promptly. "And I know Lady Rufford's diamonds are insured with a Bristol agent—one of my grandfather's old friends."

"Your grandfather was a businessman, then?" Richard turned his gaze back to Miss Burnley, feeling curious despite her rejection. She had told him very little about her immediate family, or even about her relationship with the Ruffords. He knew she called Lady Rufford "Aunt," but he could have sworn that Lady Rufford had described Miss Burnley as a distant cousin rather than her literal niece.

"Yes. I mean—Miss Rufford's grandfather. I call him Grandfather too, because I grew up as part of the family. But really, he is only a distant relation." Her lips tightened, her cheeks flushed, and she looked steadily in front of her, no longer meeting Richard's eyes.

Richard drew his brows together, confused. What she said fit the story he had heard from Lord and Lady Rufford, but he did not believe it. He could not have said why, but he felt fairly certain that Miss Burnley was once again lying to him. *It is none of my business*, he reminded himself. If there was a mystery about Miss Burnley's family tree, he had no right to inquire about it.

"I see. Thank you for telling me. I had not even considered that the jewels might be insured." That was a weight off both Richard's mind and his pocketbook. He had no idea what a full parure of diamonds cost, but he knew he would have struggled to cover the cost. And that did not even begin to address the missing rubies and emeralds.

He still hoped to recover the jewels. Insurance might make up for the monetary loss, but it did not extend to the sentimental value of the jewelry. Family heirlooms were often tightly bound to family history. Simply replacing a set of diamonds or emeralds could not restore the lost connection to the past.

Unfortunately, the Bow Street Runner would not get here until after the New Year, and Richard feared that would be too late. The original plan had been for the house party to last until Twelfth Night, when Richard would host a ball for the neighboring gentry. But some of the guests now spoke of leaving early. And who could blame them? Staying longer might mean risking more losses!

This really was a failure of a house party, wasn't it?

Chapter Ten

I T BROKE IVY'S heart to be cold to Lord Inglewhite when he had clearly been disposed to treat her with friendliness. Or possibly something warmer than friendliness. After the debacle of the kiss on Christmas Day, she hoped a lack of positive encouragement would be enough to send the right message. Throughout the week between Christmas and New Year's, she forced herself not to either look across the table to meet his eyes when they dined or to smile too broadly when she did look at him.

Despite her withdrawal, he continued to seek her out during walks, rides, and after-dinner social hours. If she sat near the pianoforte to listen to Rose playing Christmas carols, he sat next to her and spoke to her about the music. If, instead, she curled up in a corner next to a lamp and read a book, he would drift her way with a book of his own and read near her in silence. He did not flirt outrageously, the way some of her past suitors had done, nor did he shower her with unwanted compliments. But he quietly made it clear that he enjoyed her company and wanted to know her better.

On the thirtieth of December, the Rufford women had a rare moment to themselves, chatting in Rose's room while their maid arranged Rose's hair in perfect ringlets. Ivy wore her hair straight today, swept up into a smooth, tidy knot.

Aunt Rufford shook her head at this restrained hairstyle. "You look pretty, but you want a touch to enliven that coiffure. You ought to have a tiara. It would suit your hair. And your face!"

"A tiara?" Ivy giggled at the startling image. "Me? That will never happen." What a waste of money it would be!

"You never know." Rose gave her a sly, sideways glance. "The Selwyn family might very well have a tiara. They have lived in this castle for generations, haven't they? They have probably accumulated centuries of fine jewelry."

Ivy rubbed her hands together nervously, not liking this turn in the conversation. "The Inglewhite jewels have nothing to do with me." Her voice shook, though she tried to sound cheerful and confident.

"Really, my dear," Aunt Rufford said, "there is no need to be missish. Lord Inglewhite has shown a marked preference for your company during this visit. It may come to nothing, so you do well not to raise your hopes too much, but you never know. We might see you a countess yet." She beamed happily.

Ivy stared down at her clasped hands. "I am not fit to be a countess," she whispered. "You know that."

Aunt Rufford's smile fell. "You have a very generous dowry, a good education, and your uncle and I raised you like our own daughter. You would be fit to be a duchess!" She lifted her chin at a determined angle.

Ivy chuckled bitterly at the thought of her becoming a duchess. Then she leaned forward and kissed her aunt on the cheek. "That is a pretty dream, Aunt Rufford. And a pretty compliment to me. But even if Lord Inglewhite did offer for me, I would refuse him."

"But what if he did not mind your background?" Rose asked. "He seems very kind. And I suppose he is good looking for a man of his age." Her doubtful tone and the way she wrinkled her nose suggested she herself did not find the earl attractive.

Ivy, having seen her cousin's taste in men, was not surprised. Rose liked gentlemen with lively spirits, full of witty quips or gallant compliments. Lord Inglewhite's gravity and thoughtfulness were not likely to appeal to her.

"I am sure Lord Inglewhite means only to keep himself amused during the house party. I am glad he finds me agreeable, but it will all come to nothing." Ivy hoped her smile looked more convincing than it felt. She did not believe her own words.

At the back of her mind, she could still hear Lord Inglewhite telling her he *did* mean something by kissing her, that he did not play games with women. Aunt Rufford might be right that a coronet could be Ivy's for the asking. But it would be better if Aunt Rufford did not set her heart on the match. Ivy would only bring dishonor to the Selwyn name.

Once again, she longed to go home. That would be the best way to avoid any further entanglements, wouldn't it? But her uncle and aunt would never consider cutting their visit short, since it would disrupt Lord Francis's courtship of Rose. Ivy had no desire to put a spoke in that wheel either. On the contrary, she had been doing her best to subtly promote it. Lord Francis was a charming man, and Rose deserved her chance at happiness.

In any case, only one week of the visit remained. Ivy could survive another week. But she would have to be colder to Lord Inglewhite. Instead of merely ignoring him, she would have to snub him.

Therefore, the New Year's Eve ride along the river, which would have delighted Ivy under other circumstances, felt like torture. She responded to Lord Inglewhite's questions with the shortest answer possible, avoiding eye contact. Looking out of the corner of her eye, though, she could see that he looked hurt. By the end of the ride, he too had fallen silent.

She returned to the castle to dress for dinner, feeling guilty for having treated Lord Inglewhite with the same cold indifference she would have shown to a bounder or roue who paid her unwanted attention. She could not even comfort herself with the belief that he had been uninjured by the treatment, because she could hear the unhappiness in his voice when they parted. Her heart ached, because it felt very wrong to snub so kind a gentleman. But sometimes, as the bard said, one had to be cruel to be kind.

That night, most of the guests stayed up playing cards until the clock struck twelve. They toasted the New Year with a sweet, spicy punch. Then the party dispersed. Ivy, who had been wearing her birthday pendant, put it in her jewelry box. Then, just to be certain, she patted the little velvet pouch that held the signet ring, checking if the ring was safe.

The bag was empty. A sharp pain lanced through her heart, and her mouth fell open in shock. Could she have simply misplaced the ring? She pulled the bag out of her jewelry case and turned it inside out, as if it were possible for the enormous ring to be somehow hidden in a corner. But there was nothing inside the bag. She frantically searched the rest of the jewelry box, but could not find the missing ring.

Had the jewel thief taken it? But why? It could not be worth very much money. And it made no sense to take the signet ring and leave her pearl necklace behind. Wouldn't the pearls have been more valuable? That necklace still rested in its proper place, untouched. Only her father's ring had been taken.

Ivy began to shake. She could have more easily spared any-thing else from her meager jewelry collection. Why the ring? Though her feelings about her unknown father were complicat-ed, to say the least, the signet ring had still been one of her most precious possessions. Now it was gone. Tears pricked at her eyes, but she blinked them away. She could not afford to waste time crying. She had to find that ring.

Ivy could not possibly sleep with so much on her mind, so she did not even try. She spent half an hour pacing back and forth in her bedroom, until she grew chilly. These guest rooms did not have fireplaces, so the guests relied on bedwarmers and thick blankets to ward off the chill. The sensible thing to do would be to curl up under the blankets and go to sleep. But she felt far too restless for that. She had to *do* something, right now. But what?

She looked down at the still-flickering candle on her dressing table. At this hour, the house would be quiet. Even the servants would be abed for the night. But there had been a comfortable fire in the drawing room less than an hour ago. Odds were, it had not yet died all the way. It would be warmer there. She could pace and scheme to her heart's content without disturbing anyone. She took her candle and crept downstairs, treading quietly so as not to disturb any of the sleeping guests.

The open door of the library foiled her plan. A flicker of candlelight danced in the room, and without thinking, she glanced inside. Lord Inglewhite sat at his desk, writing something with a quill pen. Like her, he still wore his evening clothes. She meant to tiptoe past him on her way to the drawing room, but he happened to look up at the wrong moment. Their eyes met across the dimly lit room.

"Miss Burnley! What are you doing up?"

"Thinking. I could not sleep." Though that did not explain why she was still fully dressed. It must be obvious that she had yet to get ready for bed.

But he seemed to accept the answer. "Ah, I know that feeling." He put down his pen and shook his hand, stretching out fingers cramped from writing. "Is there anything I can do to help?"

She frowned and twisted her fingers together nervously. Then she stepped into the room, approaching his desk so that she could speak to him more privately. "I don't want to add to your burdens, but you should probably know that the jewel thief seems to have taken a signet ring from my jewelry box."

"A signet ring?" He furrowed his brow and looked off to the left, as if trying to remember something. "You mean the ring from your father's family?"

"Yes." Her tightening throat made it hard to speak. "That one. The thief did not take anything else. Just that." She blinked her eyes quickly, not wanting to break down in tears in front of the earl.

"I am so very sorry. I am sure it must mean a great deal to

you." Even in the dimly lit room, she could see the concern written on his face.

"You have no idea. It is the only thing I have of my father's." She clasped her hands together, attempting to steady herself as she faced the immensity of that loss.

"He left nothing else?" Lord Inglewhite sounded surprised, and no wonder. This did not at all fit with the story the Ruffords told of Ivy's father being a country solicitor who died in a carriage accident. Had that been true, her parents would have left behind some personal possessions, if not a fortune.

Ivy drew a deep breath. Perhaps she was still tipsy from the punch she had drunk at midnight. Or maybe the lateness of the hour skewed her thinking. She knew only that she longed to confide in someone, and Lord Inglewhite's kind face suggested he might be a trustworthy listener.

"If I tell you a secret," she said slowly, "will you keep it in confidence?"

"Of course," he said at once. "As a clergyman, I have often had to keep other people's secrets. A vicar of the church of England may not be bound by the seal of confession the way a Romish priest would be, but I take all confidences quite seriously."

Ivy nodded and squeezed her hands together more tightly. How should she begin this story? What could she tell, and what must she conceal?

"Why don't you come and sit down by the fire?" He gestured toward a pair of high wooden settles on either side of the hearth. "You must be cold."

"Yes," Ivy agreed. "It is a chilly night."

There was something dreamlike about the way she moved through the shadowy room and took her seat on the padded cushion of the settle. It was as if her mind were separated from her body, and she merely watched herself go through the motions of sitting down, adjusting her skirt, and crossing her legs at the ankles. None of it felt real. Was she really about to spill her darkest secret to a man who wanted to court her?

The dwindling fire still cast light and warmth on this side of the dim room. She set her candle down on the wide, flat wooden arm nearest her. Then she rested her hands in her lap. She looked down and saw, to her surprise, that her fingers were intertwined, lying still and motionless together. Internally, Ivy jittered so much that she had expected her body to physically tremble in response, but that was not the case.

Lord Inglewhite sat at the other end of the settle, leaving at least a foot of space between them, for which Ivy was grateful. Being here alone with him made her nervous. An unmarried lady and an unmarried gentleman ought not be alone together so late at night without a chaperone. But, on the other hand, he was not listening to her in the role of a potential suitor. She meant to confide in him as if to a priest, though it was not her own sin she would confess.

"You must keep this story in strictest confidence, because it reflects poorly not only on me, but on my mother's whole family. My grandparents went to some trouble to hush the matter up twenty-five years ago. I do not want their work to go to waste."

"I will keep your secret. But what is it?" He looked across the length of the settle into her eyes, his expression as earnest as she had ever seen it.

Now that it came down to the moment of truth, Ivy found it hard to talk. She looked away from Lord Inglewhite, staring into the dying fire. Her mouth felt dry. For a moment, she considered telling him she had changed her mind and did not want to share her secret. But perhaps, given the circumstances, he had a right to know her history. Once he heard the story, he would understand why she could not encourage his suit.

She drew a deep breath, let it out slowly, and closed her eyes, hoping that would make it easier to speak. "The story you have heard about my parentage and birth is false. I was raised by my Aunt and Uncle Rufford, but my mother did not die when I was a baby. Nor was she Lady Rufford's distant cousin. My mother was

Mercy Haworth, Lady Rufford's older sister."

Lord Inglewhite wrinkled his brow in confusion. "I thought Lady Rufford's sister married a gentleman in Berkshire. Did she have another sister?"

"No." Ivy swallowed uneasily. "That was my mother. She married a gentleman farmer, Mr. Brown. She had three other children before she died. My half-siblings."

Her brothers and sister would never know the truth about their relationship because her mother had made Ivy promise to keep it a secret. Mr. Brown knew the truth, but he had been sworn to silence, too. He was an honorable man and would take the secret to his grave.

Ivy drew a deep breath before she said the hardest part. "I was born before she married Mr. Brown, and she never even knew my father's identity."

She looked up from the fire to see how Lord Inglewhite reacted to this revelation. His brows were creased in concern, but he seemed to be patiently waiting for her to say more. If he felt scandalized by her tale, he hid it well. As a clergyman, he might well have heard worse things. That gave her the courage to continue the story.

"My mother met my father at a masquerade, in a public assembly hall. Since it was not a private party, he could have been anyone. My mother knew only that he was well-spoken and well-dressed." She swallowed uneasily as she recalled the few details her mother had given her. "He was costumed as a highwayman."

She had always thought his costume was fitting, given the way he had robbed her mother of the future she might have expected. Mercy Haworth's father had been only a Bristol merchant, but he was rich as Croesus. Miss Haworth's dowry of fifty thousand pounds might have allowed her to marry well despite her middle-class birth . . . if she had not been seduced by a stranger at a public ball.

"And they, er, had a tryst?" Lord Inglewhite suggested delicately.

She nodded. Her mother refused to say much about it, so Ivy had no idea how or why she had given her virtue to a man whose name she did not even know. Perhaps alcohol had been involved. Perhaps Miss Haworth had been carried away by the spirit of license a masquerade created. Or so Aunt Rufford had suggested. Ivy had never been to a masquerade herself, so she took that description on faith.

All Ivy knew was that she had been conceived in a storage room or closet or some such corner in the building that housed the public assembly rooms. She could imagine no more sordid a beginning. Whoever her father had been, whatever his rank in life, he could not have been a true gentleman.

"He lied to her when he seduced her," she said, silently hating the unknown man. "He told her that he would come back and find her, that he would do the honorable thing by her. He gave her his signet ring as a pledge. But she never saw him again."

Lord Inglewhite frowned. "Couldn't she have used the ring to track him down?"

Ivy looked down at her lap and saw, rather to her surprise, that she had been pleating her skirt nervously. She tried to smooth the skirt out with sweat-dampened hands. She had never told anyone this story before. Perhaps that was what made it so hard.

"Yes," she agreed. "Mother could very likely have tracked him down by the coat of arms on the ring. But she refused to do so. She always said that a man who would abandon her was not worth finding again."

Ivy sighed. She understood her mother's decision but was not sure she agreed with it. So long as her father's identity remained unknown, questions about him would always lurk at the back of Ivy's mind. Now her mother was gone, but after so many years, it was probably too late to uncover any answers.

Fortunately, the rest of the story was easier to tell. "My grandfather was quite well-to-do, so there was no need of financial support from my father, you understand. Grandfather could afford to hush things up. My mother went away to the seaside for her health and did not come back until after her confinement ended. My aunt had married Lord Rufford—though he was not the baron yet—a year before, and the family decided the Ruffords should raise me. So, they concocted the story about my parents dying in an accident and treated me as if I were a distant but beloved cousin."

That was one thing to be grateful for: Ivy had never known a moment without love. Her aunt and uncle loved her and had reared her as if she were their own daughter. Her grandparents had doted on her, treating her no differently from their other grandchildren. Her mother had loved her dearly, too, though after she married Mr. Brown, they only saw each other a few times a year.

Ivy drew a deep breath and continued her story. Her throat had grown dry from talking, and she found herself longing for a cup of tea or a glass of wine. "After my mother married, there was some talk of sending me to live with her and her new husband. She told him the truth about her past, and he would have taken me in. But by that time my aunt and uncle were very attached to me. And my stepfather, though a good man, did not move in the highest social circles. My mother thought it would be to my advantage to be raised in Lord Rufford's manor rather than in Mr. Brown's farmhouse."

Ivy was not sure she agreed with this, either. She had always loved Rufford Manor and the family she had there, but she could not help regretting the separation from her mother. Mr. Brown would have been a kind stepfather to her. Although he was not wealthy, he owned his own farm and enjoyed a comfortable life. Life at Restharrow Farm would have had many joys, even if it lacked some of the luxuries of Rufford Manor.

Ivy's mother had believed growing up in an aristocratic household might mitigate the shame of Ivy's birth. But Ivy, who understood the aristocracy better than her middle-class mother ever had, knew nothing could wash away the stain of illegitimacy.

It might have been better had she been reared in a less exalted station of life, with more modest expectations. Perhaps she would have been happier in the long run. She might even have found a suitor who would not mind her scandalous background.

Ivy cleared her throat and tried to put those regrets aside. There could be no going back to change the past now. "Anyway, that is the true story. I was twenty-one when my mother passed away, so I grew up knowing her. But all I had of my father was his signet ring. And now someone has taken even that from me." She closed her eyes as the pain of the theft hit her anew.

"We will get it back." Lord Inglewhite spoke softly, but his voice rang with quiet confidence. "Even if it means tearing down every stone of the castle to find it. I will not allow someone to rob you of so precious a legacy."

Ivy's mouth curved into a rueful smile. "It is not worth the trouble, my lord. And I am sorry to burden you with so much unwanted knowledge. I just thought you should know the thief struck again. And I thought you should know . . ." She did not know how to finish that sentence. Maybe she should simply stop there.

"Thought I should know what?" His voice was soft and reassuring, and he met her gaze confidently.

She could imagine no man less threatening than Lord Inglewhite. Even so, she feared she was about to make a terrible mistake. She darted her eyes away from his face, staring instead at the glowing embers in the fireplace. She hoped to find some courage there. His lordship deserved to know the whole truth, didn't he? She drew a deep breath and squared her shoulders.

"I thought you should know that my background is the reason why I . . . why I am not looking to marry. I intend to remain a spinster, because I do not want to poison any other family with my disgrace."

She had meant to say, "my mother's disgrace," but somehow the words became garbled. Well, it amounted to the same thing, didn't it? Her mother's disgrace was hers, because the sins of the father were visited on the children.

The corners of Lord Inglewhite's mouth turned down at this. "I see." He studied the tips of his own shoes for a moment, then cleared his throat. "Is that why you have been discouraging me?"

"Yes." Ivy did not trust herself to say anything more. If she opened her mouth again, she might say something she would regret. She closed her eyes, relieved to have that out between them.

Now Lord Inglewhite could turn his attention elsewhere. Would Miss Canning suit him? She was younger than Ivy, but she had already had a few seasons and had not "taken." Miss Canning seemed rather shy, but so kind a man as Lord Inglewhite ought to be able to thaw the chill of her reserve. Perhaps Ivy could give her some encouragement? Now that Rose's romantic affairs seemed to be in good order, perhaps Ivy could spare some time to help less fortunate guests find partners.

Lord Inglewhite interrupted Ivy's matchmaking plans. "Don't you think," he suggested, "you should leave it up to your suitor to decide whether your background constitutes an insurmountable obstacle to matrimony?"

Ivy's eyes widened and her breath hitched. After hearing the whole sordid story, he could not mean to imply what it sounded like. Could he?

Chapter Eleven

M ISS BURNLEY (OR ought it be Miss Haworth?) stared at Richard, her eyes widening with surprise. "I have not the pleasure of understanding you, sir," she said doubtfully.

Richard took a deep breath before speaking, knowing he skated on thin ice here. "I mean that not all gentlemen would object to you as a marriage partner, even knowing about your illegitimacy."

He paused, not certain he should say more. On the one hand, he had only known her two weeks, so it seemed premature to make an official offer of marriage. On the other hand, she would only be a guest at the castle for one more week. The Ruffords planned to leave the Monday after the Twelfth Night ball. That did not leave much time for Richard to convince Miss Burnley (he had better stick to her assumed name) to reconsider her position on matrimony.

She looked away from him, her mouth tightening into a grim line. "Perhaps there are some gentlemen who would not mind it. But it would not be right to bring such . . . shame . . . into a *noble* family line." Her voice wavered as she spoke. "If I were being courted by a man of a less exalted station, who did not have so great a duty to maintain his family name, it might be a different matter."

Richard sighed. Yes, this conversation was going to require all his tact. "Again, I think it would be best if you allowed your prospective husband to decide what would or would not corrupt his family line. Most noble families already contain a few b— illegitimate people in their family trees." He tensed up, realizing he had nearly used an unforgivable insult in discussing his prospective bride. "My great-grandmother, for instance, was supposed to be the by-blow of the Duke of Cambridge." Though no one had ever known for certain whether that rumor was true. His great-great-grandmother had been married to the Marquis of Camborne at the time and it could have been his child after all.

"I very much doubt my father was a royal duke in disguise." Miss Burnley smiled wryly as she gazed into the fireplace, though he could see little there to draw her eye. Only embers smoldered in the grate. "All sorts of people attended those masquerades. He might have been a man of business, like my grandfather. Or an industrialist. Or the son of a local squire." She shrugged her shoulders. "Or anyone, really."

Anyone willing to seduce and abandon a girl at a masquerade, Richard silently qualified. That must rule out a good many people. Unfortunately, you could not tell by looking at a man whether he was capable of such behavior. And sometimes gentlemen who were wild in their youth settled down and became respectable in their middle years, so her father might not be known as a rake today. A man could change a great deal over a quarter of a century.

"What did the signet ring look like?" Richard asked. That might provide a clue as to the unknown seducer's identity.

"The stone was black and white, made of sardonyx," she explained. "And the coat of arms depicts a winged lion sitting on an open book."

Richard stiffened. He knew that heraldic device. He had seen it when the first group of houseguests arrived, blazoned on the carriage used by the Marchioness of Reading. "You are certain of the design?" He studied her face intently as he turned a new idea around in his mind.

She stared back at him, looking surprised again. It had, he supposed, been a rather foolish question. Of course, she would be certain of the emblem! Since it was the only clue she had to her father's identity, she had probably memorized every scratch or blemish on the ring.

"Yes, very sure. I showed it to our vicar once, and he said the winged lion was the symbol of St. Mark."

"Yes, it is," Richard agreed. "But it is also . . ." He paused, feeling he ventured into murky waters. "I have seen it used as part of a coat of arms." The winged lion alone might not be uncommon in heraldry, but there could not be more than one family whose coat of arms consisted of a winged lion on an open book, could there?

"Really? Whose coat of arms is it?" She leaned forward slightly, nervously biting her lip.

Richard studied his own clasped hands as he tried to work out what he could and could not say. Murky waters, indeed! "I am not sure I should tell you. I think I need to do some investigation first."

He had to balance Miss Burnley's natural desire to know her father's identity with his obligations as a host. He did not want to stir up scandal unless he had to. If the Marquis of Reading himself had been at the house party, Richard would have confronted him directly to ask if he were responsible. But Lord Reading's health had declined over the last few years. He no longer traveled far from home.

But it made sense, didn't it? Everyone knew the Marquis of Reading had been wild and rakish in his youth. He had been precisely the sort of young man who would go slumming at a public masquerade, tumble a merchant's daughter, and then carelessly abandon her. If he had promised to marry Miss Haworth, it would have been an empty promise, since he was already married to the current Marchioness.

The only thing that did not fit was the signet ring itself. A young nobleman would not have given away so personal a possession unless he intended to retrieve it later. If a man meant to seduce a girl and then flee the consequences, he would hardly leave behind a piece of jewelry that could identify him by his coat of arms! But that objection would apply to anyone, not just the Marquis of Reading. Richard found it hard to understand how the ring could fit into the most likely scenarios.

Richard studied Miss Burnley's face again, searching for signs that she might be related to the Bracknell family. She did not resemble Lord Crowthorne much, so far as he could tell by the flickering candlelight, but her auburn hair was very much the same color as Lord Francis's. He had noticed that before and thought nothing of it. But now, in light of his knowledge about the coat of arms, it seemed a significant clue.

"I had rather not share my suspicions until I have done some investigation," he said again, repeating himself as if to reassure them both.

He would have to write to the Marquis of Reading. He did not look forward to composing *that* letter. He knew the Bracknell family primarily through the Marchioness, who was a distant cousin on his mother's side of the family. But he and Lord Reading were not on such terms as to discuss past romantic indiscretions with each other. Not that Richard had any such indiscretions to discuss!

"I will look into this, Miss Burnley," he promised.

She shook her head. "You need not trouble yourself on my account."

Richard lifted his brows, surprised. "Are you not curious about your father's identity? Would you not rather know your family history?" If he were in her shoes, he could not imagine turning down the chance to answer a lifelong question.

She shrugged. "I know the Haworth family story, and the history of Rufford Manor. Those are the places and people I belong to. I have no need of financial support from my father, even if he were willing to provide it. My grandfather left me a very generous fortune."

Richard frowned. "Do you wish me to investigate, or not?" If she preferred not to know, he would respect her wish and refrain from digging further. Though he would always have suspicions, knowing what he did now.

Miss Burnley twined her fingers together, squeezing them tightly. She remained quiet for a moment, thinking. "I suppose if you learn anything about the coat of arms or the original owner of the ring, I would like to know it, too." She darted a cautious glance in his direction. "But you need not put yourself out on my account."

"I will see what I can do. And when the Bow Street Runner gets here, I will tell him about the missing ring." It might not be as costly as the stolen sets of jewels, but its personal significance clearly extended beyond its material value.

She stood up to take her leave. Richard felt a pang of disappointment, as if he had expected her to linger here a little longer with him. But that was absurd. It was well past midnight, and the whole house had gone to sleep. The room had grown colder as the fire died down, too. Miss Burnley must feel chilly without a shawl to warm her.

Richard felt there were things he ought to say, but he did not know what they were. He rose to his feet slowly, hoping to find the perfect words buried amongst his muddled thoughts. Unfortunately, he discovered no hidden gems of eloquence, so he had to fall back on commonplace courtesy.

"Thank you for your confidence, Miss Burnley. I will keep your identity secret as I make my inquiries." When he wrote to the Marquis of Reading, he would have to conceal Miss Burnley's name. But that should be easy enough to do.

"I appreciate your discretion, my lord." She inclined her head in farewell and turned to go.

"Wait!" He had finally thought of a further question.

She turned back to look at him, her mouth ajar with surprise.

"Perhaps this does not matter, but do you by any chance know what costume your mother wore at the masquerade?" If her father never revealed his name, Miss Haworth might have kept her name a secret from her lover, too, in which case he would only know her by her costume. Though, in that case, how would the unknown gentleman come back to find the girl with whom he had trysted? The pieces of the story did not hang together properly yet.

The confusion on Miss Burnley's face cleared away. "Oh, yes, you might need to know that. She came garbed as a shepherdess."

"A shepherdess," Richard repeated. "Very well. That is all." He could think of nothing more to say to keep her with him longer—and why should he try to detain her, anyway? It was scandalous for them to meet alone at night. "I will inform you if I learn anything," he promised. So they parted, though Richard felt he had not said half the things he wanted to say.

The next morning, before he did anything else, he wrote to the Marquis of Reading. True to his word, Richard did not reveal Miss Burnley's name or her connections. But he described the encounter at the masquerade as best he could, and he wrote down everything Miss Burnley had told him about the missing ring. Even if Reading had *not* been the stranger at the masquerade, he might have some idea who else would have worn such a signet ring.

The day after that, the Bow Street Runner finally arrived. He quickly turned the entire castle upside down in his search for the missing jewels. Richard tried to explain that they had already searched everywhere, but the Runner, a man by the name of Davies, had his own method. He insisted on going over everything again—a matter that could take days. Davies was paid by the day, and Richard cynically wondered if he intended to take his time looking for the jewels so as to increase his pay.

Time proved Richard's suspicions wrong. The second day, early in the morning, Davies came to the library door, hat in hand. A triumphant smile lit up his face. "My lord, I 'ave somethin' to show you. Come with me, if you please."

Richard followed the Runner out of the castle and into the

carriage house. Carriages belonging to the guests packed the building. Some of the Selwyn vehicles had, in fact, been moved to a distant barn to make room for the guests. Davies led Richard through a maze of vehicles to an old-fashioned traveling coach. Richard did not recognize the vehicle, and he did not have time to check the coat of arms, because Davies opened the door and gestured for Richard to climb inside.

Inside the coach, the padding on the back of one seat had been pulled out. The apparent damage horrified Richard until he saw that the squab was made to be removed. A little hollow space had been built behind the cushion. A pile of velvet bags rested inside the cavity.

"The jewels?" Richard asked hoarsely.

No wonder the servants had not found them when they searched the castle! No one would think to look for a secret storage space inside a coach. No one but a carriage designer, perhaps, or a trained investigator like Mr. Davies. Even the magistrate had not thought of such a thing.

"Take a look for yourself, m'lord." Davies spoke respectfully, but his face radiated quiet triumph.

Richard investigated the contents of the velvet bags. The first one held rubies, the second diamonds, the third emeralds. The last bag had little odds and ends: the silver fish forks, Richard's missing sapphire stickpin, other small items. But no signet ring, strangely enough.

"Whose carriage is this?" he demanded.

Davies shook his head. "You would know better than I, m'lord. There's a coat of arms on th' door, but it means nothing to me."

Richard stepped back and peered at the emblem on the door. It bore an elephant with a howdah on its back.

"That is Sir Michael Canning's coat of arms." The Cannings had made their fortune in the East India Company, and when Sir Michael's father was elevated to the rank of baronet, he chose a coat of arms to reflect his past. "Does that mean someone from the Canning family took the jewels?" Richard had trouble believing that.

"As to that, it is too early to tell," Davies said sagely. "I would like to speak to all the members of the family."

Richard nodded. "Yes, I will arrange that." That was the logical next step.

But the discovery did not make sense. Those gorgeous rubies were Canning family heirlooms. Why would a member of the family steal them? And who from the family would need to steal at all? Sir Michael was flush with money, so far as Richard knew. He gave his heir a generous allowance, and Miss Canning did not seem to want for pin money. Neither of the young people seemed at all likely to have accrued debts of honor, though Richard supposed that possibility could not be ruled out.

Most of all, though, he wondered why Miss Burnley's signet ring had not been in the cache. That troubled him. He could not think of any reason why it would have been kept separate from the other booty. Unless . . .

"Mr. Davies, is it possible someone with no connection to the Canning family hid the jewels here to throw us off the scent?"

"Aye, it's possible," the Runner admitted. "But it'd have to be someone who knew about the hiding place. A member of the family or a servant is more likely. But we cannot rule anyone out."

So, they had found the jewels, but the hunt was not over. Now they had to catch the thief.

Chapter Twelve

The whole tenor of the house party changed after the discovery of the jewels. Lady Rufford and the Marchioness of Reading were both overjoyed to have their prize possessions back. Once Lady Rufford's diamonds were restored, she ceased regretting having come to the house party. Instead, she resumed talking hopefully about Rose's prospects. Lord Francis had not declared himself, but a proposal seemed imminent.

Lady Canning, on the other hand, was furious to find her family under suspicion. After dinner, she sat next to Lady Rufford and described the indignity of being interviewed by a Bow Street Runner. She seemed ashamed that the jewels had been found in her carriage.

Ivy listened to Lady Canning's complaints with only half an ear. She found it difficult to attend to anything today, because she kept hearing, over and over again, Lord Inglewhite's words last night. She did not know which unsettled her more: the prospect of at last learning the identity of her father, or the possibility that the earl might want to marry her despite knowing the truth about her background.

He had not declared himself or made anything resembling an offer of marriage. But if he did . . . what then? Ivy had always believed it would be wrong to bring her disgrace into one of England's noble family lines. She had not considered the possibility that one of her suitors would disagree with this opinion.

Still, it changed nothing, did it? Perhaps Lord Inglewhite was a little infatuated with her. (Ivy blushed at the thought.) But if he married her, he would eventually regret it. The stigma of illegitimacy would taint not only Ivy, but any children she might have. She could not bear the thought of her children being slandered, shunned, or mocked for something they could not help.

True, Ivy had never experienced such prejudice, because her mother's family had done such a good job of covering up the scandal. But if Ivy became the Countess of Inglewhite, people would ask questions about her birth, her family, and her history. It might not be possible to keep the secret any longer. And when the truth was discovered, it would affect her husband's family as well as her mother's family.

Once his infatuation faded, Lord Inglewhite would realize he would be much better off marrying someone of impeccable background. He would be *glad* Ivy refused him. Assuming that he offered, of course, which he might not. He might have already thought better of his words last night, and—

"I wished to speak to you, Miss Burnley, about the object you misplaced."

She had been so deep in thought, she had not realized that the subject of her ruminations stood at her side. She tipped her head back to look Lord Inglewhite in the face.

"Yes? What is it?" She assumed the Bow Street Runner must be keeping her ring for some forensic purpose, though it was strange that the Runner had given everyone else their jewels back.

"Would you be so gracious as to sit with me for a moment?"

She stared at him, confused. There was an empty chair next to hers. Couldn't he sit there if he wished to speak to her? But he jerked his chin in the direction of a far corner of the drawing room. Everyone had sought seats as close to the fireplace as they could get, so no one occupied the other side of the room at all.

"You wish to be private with me?" She spoke as softly as she could, not wanting to draw attention to their conversation.

He nodded infinitesimally.

Ivy turned to her aunt and announced: "I believe I will take a turn about the room, Aunt Rufford. I feel restless tonight." She did not want to make it too obvious that she and the earl were moving to a more remote corner of the room to speak together.

"As you like, my dear." Her aunt's gaze shifted back and forth between Ivy and Lord Inglewhite, but if she had questions, she did not ask them, for which Ivy was grateful.

Ivy walked about the room twice, trying her best to look as if she merely wanted to stretch her legs after sitting still for too long. Then she found a chair as far from anyone else as possible.

Lord Inglewhite took his time meandering over to her corner of the room. He paused to talk with a few of the guests, smiling, nodding, and generally playing the part of a good host. But eventually he, too, drifted toward the colder, darker side of the room and sat next to Ivy. Somehow, she felt unnaturally aware of his presence. He sat a polite distance from her, giving her plenty of space, but his proximity altered everything about the room.

He said nothing for a moment, merely watching the crowd at the other end of the rectangular room. "This is an awkwardly designed room in many ways," he observed. "Too long to be comfortably heated by a single fire. I have always preferred the morning room and the green salon."

"It is quite elegant, though," Ivy said politely. "I suppose it must have been recently redecorated?"

Other rooms of the house displayed furnishings from previous generations, but this one looked entirely up to date. The furniture was built on slender, curving lines, with no ornate carvings or ostentatious gilt. The wallpaper displayed a floral pattern in soft yellow and bright blue, colors that worked surprisingly well together. Those shades were echoed in the upholstery and the thick Turkish carpet in the center of the floor.

"Yes, my sister-in-law had all the furniture replaced and the walls repapered when she married my brother." Lord Inglewhite let his gaze drift about the room, too. "I suppose the fashion has not changed much since then. That was only some twelve or thirteen years ago."

"Your brother must have been very young when he died." Ivy regretted her words as soon as she spoke, fearing she had touched on a painful subject.

Lord Inglewhite nodded. "He was not quite forty. A very unexpected death, and most unfortunate that he left no son to inherit after him."

Really? She could understand Lord Inglewhite regretting his brother's death. That was perfectly natural. But it sounded as if he also regretted having inherited the title. Wouldn't most gentlemen be happy to become an earl, even if they would have preferred to have their sibling still alive?

He must have seen her surprise, for he clarified: "There are great privileges that come with a title and an estate, but I was never adequately prepared for the responsibilities. I have never been much interested in politics, but now I have to attend parliamentary sessions every year. Nor did I know anything about agriculture or estate management. My brother learned all of that, but since I was destined for the church, I ignored it all."

Lord Inglewhite leaned back in his chair, looking more relaxed. "I can no longer ignore questions about pasture conditions or treatments for mastitis in dairy cattle. My stewards bring these decisions to me and expect *me* to know the proper course of action." His rueful smile invited her to see the absurdity of expecting a man trained for the church to understand animal husbandry.

Ivy smiled back. "I suppose you must have had to learn a good deal about dairy cattle when you inherited." This part of the county was predominately used for pasturing livestock rather than growing crops.

"I *still* have a great deal to learn about dairy cattle! Please do not tell my steward how little I understand about milk production or butter making." He chuckled softly, and Ivy laughed with him.

Then she sobered, remembering she had not met with him to talk about his agricultural shortcomings. "You said you had something to discuss about my missing ring, my lord?"

"Ah, yes." His face fell into serious lines. "I regret to inform you that your ring was not in the cache with the rest of the jewels."

"It wasn't?" Ivy's voice rose up in volume, causing people on the other side of the room to glance in her direction.

Blast! She had not wanted to call attention to them. Not that anyone would guess the real topic of their conversation. The other guests would all assume Ivy and Lord Inglewhite had drawn apart from the crowd to bill and coo like a pair of courting doves. Heat flushed Ivy's face as she realized how this tete-a-tete must look to outsiders.

"It was not," Lord Inglewhite confirmed. "I believe it is the only missing item yet to be found."

Ivy did her best to ignore the audience at the far end of the room and concentrate on what his lordship was telling her. "But where could it be?"

He hesitated, shifting in his chair as if the question made him uncomfortable. "I have some guesses. I hope they are wrong, because I do not like to accuse—well, suffice it to say that whoever took the ring may have recognized the signet."

"Oh." Ivy turned that idea over in her mind, examining every facet. Her stomach churned as she considered possible implications. "You don't mean to say that he . . . that my father is *here* at this house party?" she whispered anxiously. She did not feel at all ready to confront the man who had treated her mother so terribly all those years ago.

To her relief, Lord Inglewhite shook his head at once. "No. Not that. But someone—well, someone who recognizes the coat of arms might be here. Let us leave it at that."

"But even if they recognized the coat of arms, why would

they take the ring?" Ivy wondered. That was not an excuse to steal. "Or rather, why would they keep it separate from the other jewels?"

"Perhaps to return it to whoever they thought was the rightful owner?" he suggested. "All of this is conjecture, mind you. I may be wrong. I intend to ask some judicious questions." He had been looking down at his clasped hands, but now he met her gaze again. "With your permission."

Her eyes widened with dismay. "You are not going to tell anyone about me?" He had promised to keep the truth in confidence! Had she been wrong to trust him?

Lord Inglewhite shook his head again. "No! But I wonder if you will allow me to reveal what I know to Lord Rufford? There are some questions I wish to ask your uncle."

Ivy released her breath and relaxed. "He already knows everything about my past. Everything I know, that is. I have no objection to your discussing the ring with him." She could not imagine how questioning her uncle could help locate her ring, but it could do no harm.

"Very well."

He nodded, and she thought their conversation must be over. But Lord Inglewhite showed no inclination to rejoin the rest of the guests. Instead, he changed the subject to plans for the upcoming ball, now a mere two days away.

"You will have a chance to meet many of my neighbors on Twelfth Night," he told her. "Most of the locals with whom I am on visiting terms are expected to attend. It will give you a good sense of what the local society is like."

Ivy wondered, uneasily, why he thought she would be curious about the families he socialized with. Did he intend to make her an offer after all? She had rather hoped to avoid the awkwardness of having to explicitly refuse him. But she could think of no other reason why his lordship would linger here, discussing the neighboring village, the nearest market town, and the lack of any nearby public assembly rooms.

She knew she ought to get up and walk back to her aunt's side, but she did not. Instead, she stayed with the earl in that quiet corner of the drawing room. She had questions about the castle and the park, which had been improved by Capability Brown himself, many decades ago. Lord Inglewhite claimed to know no more than she did about the principles of landscape architecture, but he knew his childhood home very well, and could talk about its most beautiful features.

With every passing minute, she increasingly expected him to excuse himself and go entertain his guests. There had been some talk of cards earlier in the evening, and she thought he might finally call for the card tables. Instead, he stayed by her side chatting until the guests parted to go to bed.

Rose smirked at Ivy as they walked up the stairs to their guest rooms, a knowing look in her eyes. "You will wear the tiara yet!" she whispered before they parted.

Ivy smiled and shook her head. She did not even know if the Selwyn family owned a tiara! Still, she lay in bed for over an hour, thinking about it. Tomorrow was Thursday, and Friday was the day of the ball. The Ruffords intended to stay at Selwyn a couple of days after the ball "to recover from the dissipation," as her aunt put it. They would leave on Monday. There was not much time left in which Lord Inglewhite could propose to Ivy. Not that she wanted him to do so, of course. But she could not help wondering if he *would*.

Perhaps all this speculation was foolish. Three weeks was not enough time to come to know someone well enough for a proposal, was it? Though the rules of courtship might work differently at house parties, where people were thrown into far greater proximity than usual.

Rose and her parents certainly seemed to expect a proposal from Lord Francis, though she had known him no longer than Ivy had known Lord Inglewhite. But their situations were very different. Lord Francis was a younger son who had to work for his living, and Rose was the daughter of a nobleman. Rose's ample dowry would augment Lord Francis's income. They would be a good match from any perspective.

But Ivy, the illegitimate grandchild of a Bristol merchant, would not be a good partner for an earl. She hoped Lord Inglewhite realized that before he said something he might regret. At least, she *thought* she hoped so—except that some tiny part of her could not stop thinking about how comfortable she might have been as the Lady of Selwyn Castle, if circumstances had been different.

Chapter Thirteen

O N THURSDAY, AN icy rain prevented the castle guests from venturing out of the castle. The guests amused themselves by playing hide and seek—a game that was, naturally, instigated by Rowland. It would not have occurred to Richard to invite adults to play children's games, but it seemed to keep most of his guests amused.

Richard was grateful to his brother for entertaining his guests, but he felt too anxious to join the game himself. To him, the weather was more than a mere inconvenience. If the roads stayed icy, guests might not be able to attend tomorrow's Twelfth Night ball. Richard could not stop fretting about that. He spent a good part of the morning staring out the window, worrying about when the rain would stop. But there was nothing to be done about it. He could neither control nor predict the weather. He would simply have to wait and see.

That afternoon, when half the guests were napping, Richard summoned Lord Rufford to the library to discuss the matter of Ivy's missing ring.

"You are probably wondering why I have called you here," Richard began, knowing full well those were the most cliché words ever used to begin an important conversation.

Lord Rufford beamed. "I believe I can guess. This is about Miss Burnley, is it not?"

"Yes." Richard wondered how he knew. Had Miss Burnley warned her uncle that Richard meant to talk to him about her unknown father?

"I am her trustee, and formerly her legal guardian," Lord Rufford explained, "so you have come to the right person. Her grandfather left her a substantial dowry, you know, but we will naturally settle it on her children."

"Oh." Richard gulped. Evidently, Lord Rufford did *not* know why he had been summoned. He thought Richard had called him here to ask for permission to pay his addresses to Miss Burnley.

Richard did some fast thinking, trying to decide how to respond. He decided to use caution. "I am not at all sure that Miss Burnley returns my regard, so it may be too early to think of settlements."

Lord Rufford dismissed Richard's concern with a wave of his hand. "It is never too early to think of settlements. I know you very well, Inglewhite, so I can have no concerns about your character." He snorted, seeming amused by the idea. "I don't believe you ever so much as sowed a single wild oat."

This was of course true, and Richard knew it was nothing to be ashamed of. Even so, he wished he could sink beneath his desk and never crawl out again. He had absolutely no desire to discuss his nonexistent sexual history with Lord Rufford. But having wandered into the middle of this conversation quite by accident, he had no idea how to get out of it. He could not run out of the room in a panic. He settled for staring down at his desk as if fascinated by the smooth mahogany surface he'd seen hundreds of times.

"I intended to seek ordination." Richard hated how stiff and formal his voice sounded. "The dissipations that might have been acceptable in another young gentleman would not have suited my profession."

And he had been morally opposed to them, anyway. Even if he had not planned to be a clergyman, he could not see himself engaging in the drinking, gaming, and dallying (to use no stronger verb) that took up so much of his peers' leisure hours.

Lord Rufford waved Richard's explanation away. "Of course, of course. All very proper! As I said, I can have no doubts about your character." He cleared his throat. "Miss Burnley's lineage may not be all that could be desired for a countess, but she has been brought up and educated as if she were my own daughter. Her behavior and manners will never disgrace you."

Knowing what he did, Richard could read between the lines. Lord Rufford knew as well as Richard did that the illegitimate granddaughter of a Bristol merchant would not normally be considered an acceptable bride for an earl, though noblemen in dire need of cash might make such a marriage. Sometimes the need to refill the family coffers overrode considerations of rank and lineage.

Richard did not have the excuse of needing a fortune to justify the match. But he refused to hold the accident of her birth against Miss Burnley. That was nothing but prejudice! If not for Miss Burnley's own reservations about her parentage, he would probably have already proposed by now. He liked her, and he thought they would deal well together. She seemed a sensible, thoughtful person with good principles. And the more time he spent with her, the more he wanted to kiss her again. There would be many benefits to marrying her.

So, instead of correcting Lord Rufford's misapprehension, Richard endured a lengthy conversation about settlements, trustees, and the terms of the late Mr. Haworth's will. He doubted he really needed to know all of the latter details, but he smiled, nodded, and made appropriate noises as Lord Rufford elaborately explained what was actually a fairly simple bequest.

"I think that's everything," Lord Rufford said at last. "Have you any questions?"

"Er, not about the settlements," Richard said politely. Everything Lord Rufford wanted seemed perfectly reasonable. "But I think it only fair to tell you Miss Burnley revealed the truth about her parentage to me. I do have some questions about that."

All the color drained from Lord Rufford's face. He drew back in his chair as if trying to get away from Richard. "She told you about that? Why?"

Richard folded his hands and rested them on the desktop, trying to project more confidence than he actually felt. "She told me because someone stole her father's signet ring, and she wanted to explain why it was so important to her." He left out the part about Miss Burnley also trying to explain why she had discouraged Richard's suit. He doubted her relatives would be happy to know she had discouraged an eligible suitor because of her background.

Lord Rufford stared at Richard, his mouth gaping. Then he shut his jaw with a snap. "Ivy knows everything there is to know about her, ah, parentage. I doubt that I can tell you anything beyond what she has already told you. I know nothing about her father other than that he dressed like a highwayman and acted like a rake." The growl in his voice suggested he had never forgiven the stranger who seduced his sister-in-law.

"Did the late Miss Haworth reveal any details of his appearance apart from his costume?" Richard prompted. "Height? Coloring?"

"Ah, that is a good question." Lord Rufford rubbed his chin, then rested his head on his hand as he thought. "It has been so long, I can't remember. Let me send Lady Rufford in to speak with you. She knew her sister much better than I."

"An excellent idea." Richard liked the plan in part because it would delay the other conversation he intended to have today. He suspected *that* discussion would be even more awkward than this one. He had gone back and forth as to which member of the Bracknell family he should approach with his queries. He finally decided to begin with Lord Francis, since Richard knew him the best. Lord Francis could not have known anything about masquerade, since he was only a little older than Ivy herself, but he might very well have heard about a family member's lost signet ring. So Richard hoped, anyway.

From Lady Rufford, he learned only that the "highwayman" who had seduced her older sister was tall, dark-haired, and dark-eyed. Not only did that describe a great many people, it also sounded very much like the stereotypical description of a handsome stranger. Richard was not sure how much weight he could put on the information.

Still, those details rather surprised Richard. He had initially speculated that the current Marquis of Reading might be the stranger Miss Haworth met at the masquerade. But Lord Reading had auburn hair, much like his younger son—or like Miss Burnley, for that matter. He could not have been the dark-haired stranger who seduced Miss Haworth.

Probably that was just as well, since the Marquis had already been married by the time Ivy was conceived. If there was anything wanting to make the event more sordid, it would have been for her father to have committed adultery rather than fornication. But who could the stranger have been, if not Lord Reading? Who else could have worn a signet ring with the Bracknell family crest?

Richard intended to meet with Lord Francis before dinner so he could talk to Miss Burnley about his findings (if any) after dinner. But he reckoned without the Bow Street Runner, who wished to speak to Richard that afternoon. Davies had finished his investigation. He did not feel confident about the identity of the thief, but he said he thought it was unlikely to be any member of the Canning family.

"I spoke to all 'o them, and I'm a good hand at telling when folk are lying. I don't believe any 'o them know who put the jewels there. Their coachman knew about the hidey-hole, but 'e wouldn't have had the chance to get into the great folks' bedrooms. If 'e did it, 'e must-a been working with someone else, and I don't know who that would be."

"But the criminal must be someone who knew about the hiding place, right?" Richard pressed. Surely that narrowed down the suspects!

A scowl crossed Davies's face. "The coachman says 'e told some of the other servants about the hidey-hole after a few glasses of ale. The family didn't use it, so 'e might not have seen any need to keep it secret. Any one o' the servants at the party could've heard about it second-hand."

"I see." Richard rubbed his forehead unhappily. He felt very grateful to Davies for finding the missing gemstones, but he would have liked to have known the identity of the thief. "Is there any more that you can do here?"

Davies shook his head. He stood before Richard's desk, hat in hand, having refused to take a seat. His posture was politely deferential, but he did not look as if he were intimidated. On the contrary, he seemed confident about his ability. And no wonder! As a Bow Street Runner, he was probably one of the best thief-catchers in London.

"You're the one footin' the bill, my lord," Davies reminded him. "If you wish me to stay here longer, I will. But I dunno if I will find out anythin' more."

"We have kept you long enough," Richard told him. "My steward will give you your wages. We are very grateful for your help in restoring the jewelry to its rightful owners." All the jewels except for Miss Burnley's signet ring, that is. Richard suspected there was a good reason why the ring hadn't been with the rest of the jewels, but he would have to conduct that sensitive investigation on his own.

Richard assumed tonight's dinner table and after-dinner conversations would be about the jewelry and Davies's departure. To his surprise, though, few people seemed to have more to say about that. Perhaps the subject had already been talked to death. Or maybe no one cared about the theft now that the gems had been recovered.

Instead, all the talk was about tomorrow's ball. The servants had cleaned the ballroom and begun some of the decorating. There would be more decorating to do tomorrow. The retiring rooms at either end of the ballroom had been cleaned and readied with whatever supplies might be needed: close stools for those needing to relieve themselves, needle and thread for mending hems, and extra hairpins in case any of the ladies needed to repair their coiffures.

And, as always, people chatted about the weather. Tonight, the topic was not a meaningless pleasantry but an object of real concern. There was some doubt about how many guests from outside the castle would be able to attend the ball, given the foul weather. At least the icy rain had stopped. The roads might still be slick in the morning, but Richard hoped the afternoon sun would clear the ice—assuming the sun shone at all.

After dinner, Richard did his best to play the part of a good host. Tonight, they had the card games that he had forgotten about yesterday. Tonight, he tried not to allow any one guest to monopolize his attention. He spoke to as many people as possible, from shy Miss Canning to the garrulous Marchioness of Reading.

But somehow, he always knew where Miss Burnley was and what she was doing. She joined one of the card tables, playing as Rowland's partner against the surprisingly lethal combination of Lord Crowthorne and Miss Canning. Richard's table was too far away for him to tell what any of them said, but he could hear a good deal of laughter. Rowland had a boisterous laugh at all times, but Richard had never heard him laugh louder than when he lost to the Crowthorne-Canning team.

After that, Miss Burnley declined to play another game. Instead, she wandered over to a window and peered out at the dark night. Richard quit pretending to ignore her and left the card table to join her. There was nothing to see out the window but blank glass, of course.

"I hope the weather cooperates for tomorrow's festivities." It was precisely the same sentiment everyone else had uttered all night, but it sounded entirely different when Miss Burnley said it. The concern in her soft brown eyes looked real.

"We will still have fun even if no one else can make it to the ball," Richard assured her.

Although it would be rather difficult to dance if they had no music. The musicians had to travel from Preston. If they could not make it to the castle, Richard would have to haul the pianoforte from the drawing room into the ballroom and ask one of the ladies to play dancing tunes. His lips twitched as he imagined it. How would they even get an instrument up two flights of stairs? The footmen were strong, but they were not *that* strong!

No, he remembered, there was a pianoforte in the schoolroom, too. It had been added a few years ago for the use of Robert's two daughters. The countess and her family left the instrument behind after Robert's death, when they moved to Blackpool for the benefit of the sea air. It should be possible to move that instrument into the ballroom, since the schoolroom was also on the third floor. All would not be lost!

"You look as if you have thought of something pleasant, my lord," Miss Burnley observed.

"I might have solved an imaginary problem," he explained. There really had been no reason for him to worry so much, after all. The musicians might arrive on time tomorrow. For all Richard knew, the weather might change overnight.

A smile flashed across her face. "Imaginary problems are the easiest to solve. Real problems do not yield so readily."

"You may be right about that," he agreed. He drew a deep breath and took the plunge he had spent all evening contemplating. "Miss Burnley, if it were not a cold night in January, I would suggest we take a walk on the terrace. Would you care to walk along the gallery instead?"

She stared at him, wrinkling her brow in confusion or concern—he could not tell which. "You mean, as part of a walking party?" she suggested.

"No," he said quietly. "I mean you and me. There are things I wish to say to you."

Her eyes widened a little. He could imagine all of the objections that must be crossing her mind. It would be improper for them to be alone in a room so far from the other guests, for one. For another, people would speculate about their absence. Their exit together might give rise to rumors of an incipient engagement.

For once, Richard hoped rumor would prove to be true.

Chapter Fourteen

IVY GAZED OUT the drawing room window, though she could see nothing but the reflection of the burning candles. She and Lord Inglewhite had already spent enough time together to give rise to all sorts of conjectures. It would not be wise to leave the room with him. But if he had news about her ring—or about the identity of her father—she wanted to hear it.

Could they find a way to meet without anyone knowing? Ivy had never been in the habit of making assignations with eligible suitors, but she seemed to be doing a lot of that at Selwyn Castle. Hopefully tonight's meeting would be the last one necessary. She did not want to inadvertently encourage her aunt's matchmaking hopes.

"I will go up to my room to fetch a shawl, then linger in the gallery," she told Lord Inglewhite. "You can meet me there in ten minutes."

"Very well." He nodded to her, then moved away to talk to his brother.

Retrieving the shawl was not merely a ruse. The drawing room had been chilly, and Ivy expected the unheated gallery to be even colder. She was right about that. Even with the shawl, she shivered as she walked slowly along the gallery, studying the family portraits of several generations of Selwyns.

She paused before a painting depicting three boys and a spaniel. All three had dark hair and blue eyes, but their builds and expressions varied. The eldest son looked confident, the middle one looked anxious, and the youngest looked like he was plotting mischief. By now, she needed no one to identify the boys. This was clearly the Earl of Inglewhite with his brothers.

The sound of footsteps made her heart skip a beat. She looked over to the doorway to see Lord Inglewhite approaching. No surprise there—who else could it be? But for some reason, her heart rate accelerated as he drew near.

"Thank you for meeting me here." He stood a few feet away from her, facing the painting. If anyone walked in on them, it would appear that they were merely admiring the portrait of the Selwyn brothers. "I have always liked this portrait. The artist captured our personalities well." His tense face relaxed into a smile. "The leader"—he pointed at the oldest son—"the worrier"—he gestured towards the image of his own younger self—"and the troublemaker."

"Yes," Ivy agreed. "I see what you mean." Mr. Selwyn, the youngest brother, seemed to have kept some of his mischievous nature. It sparked out during card play and parlor games. But she wondered if Lord Inglewhite still worried too much. She covertly glanced at him now and saw his brow furrowed with concern. Perhaps he *was* still the worrier, then.

All of this was a distraction from the real purpose of their meeting, though. She took a deep breath and got to the point. "Have you learned anything about the missing ring?"

He shook his head, and the corners of his mouth turned down. "I still have inquiries to make about that." He gave her an oddly uncertain look. "I wish to speak to you about something else tonight."

"Oh?" Ivy could not imagine what else would have been important enough for him to arrange to meet her alone like this.

"Yes, I—" He paused as a coughing fit overtook him.

"I hope you are not sickening." Ivy wrinkled her brow. "It would be a shame if you had to cancel tomorrow's ball." Not to mention that a cold or flu sweeping through the house party and infecting all the guests could be more than a trifling inconvenience.

"What?" His eyes widened with surprise. "No, no, I am perfectly fine. Just a bit of dust in my throat, I suppose." He cleared his throat and looked back at the painting for a moment. "I did speak with your uncle today, as it happens."

"Oh, I see," Ivy said politely, though she did not, in fact see what he was getting at. "Did he know anything more about the identity of my father?"

Lord Inglewhite shook his head at once. "Your aunt told me a little about what the stranger looked like, which helped me rule out one of the possibilities I had considered. But, as I said, I must make more inquiries about that matter." He paused and drew a deep breath before continuing. "We spent most of our time discussing a rather different subject."

He stared at the painting as if fascinated by it, though he must have seen it many times in the last two decades. Ivy waited patiently for him to continue speaking. Whatever he meant to talk about must be a very difficult subject, because he remained silent an awkwardly long time before he finally turned to face her.

Ivy shifted too, abandoning the pretense of looking at artwork. Instead, she looked Lord Inglewhite in the eyes, steeling herself against whatever painful revelation lay in store for her.

"Miss Burnley," Lord Inglewhite said solemnly, "your uncle has given me permission to pay my addresses to you."

Earlier, Ivy's heart had skipped a beat. Now it seemed to stop beating entirely. She wanted to interrupt him before he spoke further, but her mouth had gone dry, and she was not sure she could adequately form words.

"I apologize if I am precipitate. But, as you are leaving the castle in a few days, I thought I had better, ah, seize the day and—" He sighed, and his shoulders drooped. Then, rather to her surprise, one corner of his mouth twisted up in a crooked smile. For some reason, that made her heart beat more rapidly, too. His awkward charm was completely disarming.

"Miss Burnley, I have forgotten the speech I planned to deliver tonight. I assure you that it would have been most eloquent and moving, but all the words have escaped my brain. Suffice it to say that I have enjoyed your company during this party, and I desire nothing more than to keep you by my side. Will you marry me?"

Ivy closed her eyes and covered her mouth with her hand. Her heart had resumed its proper rhythm, but her knees felt weak. Somehow, despite how obvious Lord Inglewhite's attentions had been, she had not believed it would come to this. She could not believe he was proposing to her despite knowing about her illegitimacy.

As the silence stretched out, his face grew more anxious. "You need not give me your answer now," he assured her. "We have known each other less than three weeks. I understand that may not be enough time to allow you to know your own mind."

Ivy swallowed, trying to clear her throat. "My lord, I am flattered by your offer. I have enjoyed your company very much during this visit. I wish circumstances were such as to allow me to accept your proposal, for I think we could have been happy together . . ." Her voice faltered.

Was it a mistake to admit that? Would it not be wiser to pretend that she had some objection to Lord Inglewhite—to say she disliked his person, his manners, or his character? But that would be a lie. She did like him, very much. Even now, she wished she could step into his embrace, lean her head against her shoulder, or drop a kiss against his stubbly jaw. She closed her eyes and shook her head, trying to dismiss such fantasies.

"Your answer is no, then?" He spoke gently and calmly, but when she opened her eyes, she saw pain written all over his face.

Ivy could only nod as tears prickled her eyes. Life seemed so very, very unfair. Lord Inglewhite would have made an excellent husband. She was certain of that. It would have been easy to love him, if only she had been worthy of him.

Lord Inglewhite turned back to the portrait for a moment, though Ivy doubted he really saw it. She suspected he merely wanted time to master his expression. "When you speak of circumstances preventing you from accepting my offer, do you refer to your parentage?"

Ivy nodded, relieved that he understood. Her throat still felt too tight for speech.

"I do not wish to argue with you," Lord Inglewhite continued. "But let me ask something for clarification, if I may."

"You may." She cringed at the way her voice croaked.

"If I were still the vicar of St. John's rather than the Earl of Inglewhite, would your answer be different?"

Ivy sucked in her breath sharply. "What does that matter? You are not the vicar of St. John's. You are the Earl of Inglewhite now, and you must marry a woman fit to be a countess." What good would it do to torture them both by considering possibilities contrary to fact?

"I consider *you* fit to be a countess," Lord Inglewhite replied. "Your aunt and uncle have raised and educated you to take any place in society. And, in any case, I think it more important to marry a woman who suits *me* than to choose one who suits my rank." He sighed and hung his head. "But perhaps you do not agree that we would suit."

Ivy gasped. "That is not it. I think we might do very well together, if conditions were different." She swallowed, trying to clear her throat of that painful lump. "But I am certain that if we married, you would regret it someday. It might seem easy for you to overlook my illegitimacy now, but imagine how you would feel when the stigma affected our children."

"Do you think I haven't thought of that?" He shook his head. "But that is the wrong way of looking at the matter. Any shame associated with your birth ought not attach to you, but to the man who abandoned your mother. Consider all the men of the aristocracy who keep mistresses, who leave by-blows behind after their affairs, or who mistreat their wives. Such behavior ought to leave a far greater stigma than someone's accident of birth."

"But that is not how society sees it." He had said he did not want to argue with her, but Ivy could not keep herself from arguing back. Her voice began to rise in volume. She hoped there was no one close enough to overhear them.

"That is society's fault, not yours or mine." Unlike Ivy, Lord Inglewhite kept his voice calm and level. "Miss Burnley, why do you insist on punishing me for an accident of fate?"

"I am not punishing you!"

He turned away from the painting to face her again. "Punishing yourself, then, for something that is not your fault. Why?"

Ivy stared at him open-mouthed. She was not punishing anyone! She was trying to protect him! He had grown too dear for her to allow him to be injured by marrying her.

But at the back of her mind, she remembered Lord Inglewhite saying that she ought to let her suitor decide for himself whether or not her illegitimacy constituted an insurmountable obstacle to marriage. She closed her mouth and looked her suitor in the eye. Her heart pounded and her knees felt wobbly again, but that was nothing compared to the turmoil in her mind.

She tried one last defense. "My lord, you may perhaps be a little infatuated with me." Her face burned with embarrassment at such an open reference to his feelings. "But your infatuation will not last, and when it fades, you will wish you had made a wiser choice."

Now he did raise his voice as he answered: "I am not infatuated with you! I am proposing because I believe you would make a good wife!" They stared at each other for what seemed like a painful eternity. A blush rose on Lord Inglewhite's cheekbones, too.

"I am sorry." His words sounded clipped and short. "I seem to be getting this proposal all wrong. I know the customary thing to do would be to declare myself madly in love with you and throw myself at your feet begging for you to love me back, but—"

Ivy interrupted him. "I am glad you are not behaving so foolishly. I would think less of your common sense if you did that. The kind of passion that develops in a fortnight is likely to fade quickly, too."

"Precisely." The skin around his eyes crinkled as he smiled. "I assure you, I have thought about this matter very rationally. I believe you and I could build a comfortable life together . . ." The smile faded from his face as his voice trailed off. "Dash it all!"

Ivy flinched. She had never heard him utter anything even remotely like a curse before. (Did "dash" even count as profanity?)

"My apologies," he said immediately. "I ought not use such language. Miss Burnley, I am talking nonsense. I am *not* rational where you are concerned." Once again, his cheeks flushed with embarrassment, but he continued to hold her gaze. "I will not waste your time with flowery language or strained metaphors. I will simply say that over the last two weeks, I have become fond of you. Your good sense and solid understanding attract me as much as your loveliness does. Have I any reason for hope, or ought I to walk away from you now and never speak of this again?"

Ivy looked down at the floor, staring as intently as if she expected to be tested over the pattern of the carpet. She ought to tell him to walk away. Oughtn't she? But he was not the only one who was a little infatuated. What he offered her was very tempting.

"It is not that I do not *want* to marry you," she admitted. "But I believe I would be doing wrong if I accepted your offer. Wrong to you, wrong to your children. . . ." Her voice trailed off as she imagined the life they could have had in other circumstances. If only he were still the vicar of St. John's! She could have married him then. Life as the wife of a clergyman might have suited her very well. It would have given her many opportunities to help her local community. But it was not to be. "I am very sorry, but I must decline your offer."

"I see." Lord Inglewhite practically whispered. "Very well.

You have made yourself clear, Miss Burnley. I will trouble you no more." He bowed to her, then turned and walked away.

Ivy watched him as he walked all the way to the stairs, and then down to the ground floor. Only after he had left did she press a hand to her mouth and turn away. The sick feeling in her stomach suggested that she might have just made the greatest mistake of her life.

She had turned down an offer of marriage from a good man, even though she was halfway in love with him. Maybe more than halfway. When would she ever again have a chance like that?

It is for the best, she told herself, as tears began to trickle from her eyes. Someday even Lord Inglewhite would see that she had done the right thing. Maybe someday she would even believe it herself.

She hoped that day came soon. For now, she could only grieve over what might have been.

Chapter Fifteen

I KNEW IT *would end this way*, Richard told himself as he trudged downstairs. How else could it have ended? When they spoke in the library on New Year's Eve, Miss Burnley had made it clear that she did not mean to marry anyone due to her dubious background. At least, she did not mean to marry *him*. That was what mattered most to Richard, though he also regretted that so pleasant a young lady was dooming herself to life as a spinster.

Maybe someday Miss Burnley would meet a man who swept her off her feet. A man for whom she was willing to flaunt societal expectations. A man who could make her forget the supposed shame of her birth.

But Richard was not that man, and Miss Burnley would not be his countess. He would have to seek elsewhere for a wife. Just now, though, such a task seemed well-nigh impossible. After this second rejection, he did not see how he could muster the courage to court another young lady.

Maybe he should just ask his sister-in-law to find a bride for him. Though Sophia rarely visited London, she kept up correspondence with many of her old friends. Some of them would have sisters, cousins, or friends of marriageable age to recommend. Sophia had always been reliable, too. Richard could trust her to make a good choice for him—assuming he could muster up the courage to ask her for help.

The worst of it all was that he could not afford to slink off to his room and lick his emotional wounds in peace. No, he had to return to the drawing room to bid all his guests good night. He smiled and nodded and tried to ignore the look of surprise on Lord Rufford's face when Richard explained that he did not know where Miss Burnley had gotten to.

Please, don't let the Ruffords ask any awkward questions, he prayed. A merciful Providence must have heard his prayer, for neither Lord nor Lady Rufford inquired further about the whereabouts of their niece. He supposed they would learn soon enough that she had rejected him, but he could not bring himself to discuss it now.

Naturally, Rowland realized that something was wrong. He had spent most of the evening chatting with Lord Crowthorne, but he parted from his friend and caught Richard before he could slip out of the drawing room in search of privacy.

"I say, old chap, what's wrong?"

Richard tried to dismiss his brother's concern with a wave of his hand. "Nothing much," he said. "Just crossed in love again."

"Ah." Understanding flashed across Rowland's face, replaced by a look of sympathy. "I am very sorry to hear that. I thought you and Miss Burnley were getting along like a house on fire."

Richard looked away. "So did I," he said regretfully. "But she thinks otherwise."

"Do you want to talk about it over a glass of brandy?" Rowland suggested.

Richard shook his head. He longed to explain the situation to Rowland, but he had promised not to share the secret of Miss Burnley's illegitimacy with anyone.

"It is late." He made a show of looking at his pocket watch. Then he put the watch down to pick up a leather-bound notebook lying on a nearby tea table. "Isn't this yours?"

"Oh, yes." Rowland snatched it right out of Richard's hand. "That's where I jot down notes for reviews."

"Reviews? You mean for cases?" Richard repeated, feeling

confused. So far as he knew, his brother wasn't working on any legal cases at the moment. To his surprise, a faint flush rose along Rowland's cheekbones.

"Not for legal cases," Rowland clarified. "For books reviews, drama reviews, that sort of thing. I sometimes do a little writing on the side." He stared down at the floor, looking embarrassed. "No great literary works, mind you, just a little dabbling."

"Oh, I didn't know you wrote for publication. Though you were always good with a pen." In the past, Rowland used to write comic verse for special occasions—including a ridiculous rhyming toast that he had read aloud at Robert's wedding breakfast. Too bad there would be no occasion for Rowland to write such a poem for Richard!

Rowland cleared his throat. "Yes, I find I quite enjoy it, though I don't know that I could make a career out of it."

"No, I suppose not," Richard agreed. He had a vague impression that men who made a career out of writing for periodicals lived in shabby chambers on Grub Street, eking out a living one article at a time. There could be no reason for Rowland to live that way. He had a modest fortune to support him, and the chance to earn more as a barrister, if only he were willing to work at it.

"Have you any cases on at the moment?" he asked hopefully.

Rowland gulped. "Not at the moment, no. Perhaps something will turn up after the holidays. But, you know, we had better get to sleep, hadn't we?" He glanced wistfully towards the door.

"I suppose you are right." Richard could see quite clearly that Rowland did not want to discuss his legal work, or lack thereof. "We can talk later," he said, wanting his brother to know that they were not done with this conversation. As the head of the family, it was Richard's responsibility to keep an eye on his younger brother. That meant inquiring into why, exactly, Rowland did not seem to be applying himself to his legal career. But there was no need to have that conversation now. After the disappointment of tonight, Richard felt both exhausted and dispirited. He hoped a good night's sleep would put him to rights.

But he was not to get that rest just yet. When he came to his room to undress for the night, he discovered he had left his pocket watch downstairs. Under normal circumstances, he would have waited to retrieve it until the morning, as he had no desire to venture out of the comfort of his room on so cold a night. But he did not feel comfortable doing so with a thief in the house. The watch had once belonged to Robert, and to their father before that. He hoped to someday pass it on to a child of his own, assuming he eventually married. Assuming there was a woman out there who would not refuse him!

To his surprise, the drawing room was still occupied. Lord Crowthorne stood before the fireplace, staring moodily at the hot coals. He flinched when the door closed behind Richard.

"I beg your pardon," Richard said. "I did not mean to startle you."

Lord Crowthorne shrugged his shoulders and twisted his mouth into a smile. "It is your house, Inglewhite. You can enter any room you like."

Richard picked up his watch, which remained right where he had left it. Then he wavered for a moment, not certain whether to return to his room or linger to ask Lord Crowthorne about the missing ring. He had not forgotten his promise to Miss Burnley. She had rejected his proposal, but he still felt obligated to make inquiries on her behalf. This might be a golden opportunity. He had intended to approach Lord Francis with his question about the signet ring, not Lord Crowthorne. Who knew when he would again have the chance to speak to one of the Bracknell brothers alone?

"There was something I meant to ask your brother, but perhaps you can tell me instead?" Richard's uncertainty made the pitch rise at the end of the sentence.

Lord Crowthorne turned away from the hearth to face Richard. "I am not my brother's keeper. If you wish to know about

Francis's intentions towards Miss Rufford, you will have to ask him yourself."

"This has nothing to do with Miss Rufford," Richard assured him. "I merely had a question about the Bracknell coat of arms."

"Our coat of arms?" Lord Crowthorne stared at him, furrowing his brow in confusion. "It is a winged lion, sitting on an open book."

"That is what I thought." Richard chose his words carefully so as not to reveal anything he'd promised to conceal. "Do you know who in your family would own a signet ring with that emblem?"

Lord Crowthorne's back straightened, and his frown deepened. "Why do you ask?"

Richard sighed, knowing it was a fair question. "Someone I know lost a ring of great personal importance. It was an intaglio ring made of sardonyx, bearing the emblem of a winged lion resting on a book. From its description, I suspected it might have originally belonged to someone from the Bracknell family. I merely wondered if you know of any family member of yours who might have misplaced it a couple of decades ago."

Lord Crowthorne dropped his eyes, studying the carpet for a moment. Then he nodded. "Yes, I know who the ring belonged to. But why do *you* want to know?"

Richard's heart began to beat more quickly. Was he about to solve the mystery of Miss Burnley's parentage? "As I said, an acquaintance of mine lost it. That person not only wants it back, but is also curious about the object's history."

Lord Crowthorne scowled, managing to look both puzzled and annoyed at the same time. "Shouldn't the ring's owner know its history?"

"Not in this case. There is a mystery about the ring." The two men stared at each other for a long moment. "You will not tell me whose ring it was?" Richard's shoulders slumped with despair. It was frustrating to be denied the truth when he had gotten so close. What would he tell Miss Burnley?

"Only if you tell me why it is so important." Lord Crowthorne eyed Richard warily.

Richard considered. How much could he say without revealing the secret? He had promised to keep the fact of Miss Burnley's illegitimacy in confidence. But perhaps the bare bones of the story could be told without betraying that confidence.

"The ring was left as a pledge with a woman more than twenty-five years ago, by a man who treated her dishonorably. Her family would like to know the identity of the man." That ought to make the situation clear enough without identifying the injured party.

"Left as a pledge," Lord Crowthorne mused. "Yes, that would make sense."

"It would?" Richard held his breath, anxiously waiting for Lord Crowthorne to say more.

"Yes." Lord Crowthorne nodded again. "My uncle Alistair claimed to have met a woman he meant to marry, shortly before his death. He might very well have given her the ring. What you say would fit that story, and it would explain why no one could find his signet ring after his death."

"Your uncle Alistair," Richard repeated. "He was the fourth Marquis of Reading, wasn't he?"

Richard had entirely forgotten that Alistair Bracknell had still been alive twenty-six years ago. Naturally, the signet ring would have belonged to him. As the oldest son of the Bracknell family, he had inherited the marquisate at an early age. But, like Richard's own older brother, Alistair died tragically before he could father any heirs, leaving his younger brother—the current marquis—to step into his shoes.

"Yes. He died in a hunting accident when I was a child. I barely remember him, though people tell me I look much like him. But my father always said it was tragic that Alistair died just after he decided to marry and set up his nursery. We never knew what became of the ring. So, he left it with the woman he meant to marry." Lord Crowthorne turned to stare broodingly into the fire, clasping his hands behind his back.

"The woman he meant to marry is dead, too." Richard hoped it was safe to reveal that much. "But she passed the ring on to . . . to her family." He longed to tell Lord Crowthorne that his uncle had left a child behind, that the Bracknell brothers had a cousin they did not even know about, and she was right here at the castle. But that was not his secret to reveal. It would be up to Miss Burnley to decide what to do with this information.

"I see." Lord Crowthorne looked back over his shoulder at Richard. "I hope that answers your questions."

"I suppose it does." Alistair Bracknell, being dead, could never meet his daughter, nor could he ever make reparations for his actions. But Miss Burnley might be glad to know her father really had intended to return to her mother. "Thank you for your assistance." Richard turned to go.

"Wait."

"Yes?" Richard paused in mid-step and turned his head back to look at Lord Crowthorne.

Lord Crowthorne narrowed his eyes as he stared at Richard. "How came the ring—I mean, who was the woman Uncle Alistair gave the ring to?"

"I cannot tell you that," Richard said. "I am sorry, but it concerns someone else's family secret."

"Family secrets." Lord Crowthorne twisted his mouth into a bitter smile. "Every family has its secrets, I suppose, and every secret poisons what it touches."

The harshness with which he spoke rather shocked Richard. "The truth will make you free," he suggested, falling back onto his clerical training.

Lord Crowthorne laughed mirthlessly. "I have no use for preaching, Inglewhite." He lifted up his head and set his shoulders back, as if he had made a decision. "I bid you goodnight." He strode out of the room. Richard stared after him, wondering what secret had poisoned him.

Chapter Sixteen

January 5

IN THE MORNING, when Watts came to help Ivy dress, she carried a tiny parcel. "Miss Burnley, I found this outside your door." She sounded puzzled, as well she might be.

When Ivy unwrapped the parcel, she found the missing signet ring. She stared at it, surprised. She had assumed she would never see the ring again, since even the Bow Street Runner could not find it.

The parcel also contained a folded piece of notepaper. She opened it up to find a brief letter, written in a hand she did not recognize:

I retained this ring under the impression that it had been unlawfully obtained from the Bracknell family. Having learned my error, I hereby return it to you. It is unlikely that I will ever meet you again, but I leave you with best wishes for your future happiness.

Her heart turned a summersault when she came to the signature:

Your Cousin,
Crowthorne

Her cousin? She had a cousin who was heir to a marquisate? She sank down onto the nearest chair, trying to make sense of this. How did Lord Crowthorne get the ring? And how did he know she was his cousin? Had Lord Inglewhite told him? A wave of dread crept down her back. Surely not! Lord Inglewhite had promised to keep her illegitimacy a secret. She trusted him to do so. Her stomach soured as she imagined him sharing her family's skeleton in the closet with another nobleman, perhaps over a tumbler of brandy.

"Is something wrong, miss?" Watts held a green-sprigged morning dress in her hands, ready to help Ivy dress for the day.

"I need to speak to Lord Crowthorne as soon as I am dressed," Ivy announced. This could not wait until after breakfast. If he was really her cousin, who was her father? She had so many questions!

Watts gasped. "Didn't you know, Miss? He's gone."

"Gone?" Ivy gaped at her maid. "Gone where?" He must have been called away by some emergency.

Watts put down the dress and leaned forward to whisper conspiratorially. "No one knows where he went! He ran off in the middle of the night, and he left behind a note for Lord Inglewhite that seems to have upset his lordship very much. But no one knows where Lord Crowthorne went or why."

"He left in the middle of the night," Ivy mused.

She stared at the ring in her hand. The only way Lord Crowthorne could have gotten it was by stealing it, which meant he must be the jewel thief. But he had stolen jewels from the Marchioness of Reading, too, and she was his mother. Why would he steal his own family heirlooms? Surely, he would have wanted to present those to his own marchioness someday!

"In that case, I need to see Lord Inglewhite as soon as he is available," Ivy decided. Maybe he would have some of the answers she needed.

"You must dress first." Watts was nothing if not practical. "And I think we ought to curl your hair today, don't you? You want to look nice for Lord Inglewhite."

Ivy snorted. "I am not going to pretty myself for Lord Inglewhite. I have no desire to tempt him. Just arrange my hair as quickly as possible, please."

Watts sighed and shook her head, but she did as directed. It still took entirely too long to make Ivy presentable. She hurried downstairs, intent on finding Lord Inglewhite. But the butler, Gibson, solemnly informed her that his lordship was meeting with Squire Anderson in the library and could not be disturbed. Ivy's whole body slumped in disappointment at this news.

Gibson cleared his throat. "If you like, Miss, you might go and wait for his lordship in the green salon. I will send him in to speak with you when his meeting is over."

Ivy brightened at this suggestion. "Yes, that is an excellent idea."

Thus, she found herself pacing back and forth in front of a hastily lit fire in the green salon. This was the smallest of the castle's sitting rooms. It was located on the first story rather than the ground floor, and because of its size, it had seldom been used during the house party. The guests preferred to congregate in the morning room or the drawing room, both of which were larger and had been more recently furnished.

The name of the room seemed to be a misnomer, for it was decorated in shades of rose and beige rather than green. The walls were hung with floral-patterned silk, and the small sofa near the fireplace was upholstered in a similar rose color, echoed by the stiff armchair facing it.

Unlike the more public reception rooms of the castle, the green saloon seemed to have been designated for the use of the family. All the furnishings were pretty, but everything looked a bit worn, without quite being shabby. The pretty rose sofa, for example, had been made in the rococo style of the last century, with prominent seashells carved into the wooden base and feet.

It would have been a comfortable room to wait in, if not for one dreadful mistake. Ivy had not brought any needlework or reading material with her to keep her occupied, and she had no idea how long Lord Inglewhite's meeting would last. The room boasted a single low bookshelf, placed underneath the window. Ivy browsed the shelf, hoping to find something to distract her, but unfortunately, the books proved to be an extensive series on the history of whaling. She opened one volume up to find a gory description of flensing, and promptly closed the book shut with a snap.

"Someone gave my father those books, but I don't believe a single member of my family has managed to read more than one chapter before giving up."

Ivy jumped at the interruption. The door had opened nearly soundlessly, and she had not realized Lord Inglewhite stood in the doorway. He smiled reassuringly, but that did nothing to calm the beating of her heart. Was it really proper for him to meet her alone in this room? Should she have brought a chaperone?

"Why are there only whaling books in this room?" she asked. "I would have expected to find light literature here, for the ladies of the house." It seemed like a feminine space.

He chuckled. "That was my mother's doing. She disliked this room for some reason, and she only used it for visitors she did not particularly care for. She would send unwanted callers here to wait for her. She put those books in the room to make certain such visitors would be bored while they waited."

Ivy's mouth gaped for a second. "That's terrible!" Though it also seemed rather clever, in a devious sort of way.

"She had a rather wicked sense of humor," he admitted. "Rowland takes after her far more than I do. I ought to remove those wretched books, though. I have always liked this room. I ought to make it more habitable." The smile fell away from his face. "How can I help you, Miss Burnley?"

All at once Ivy felt the awkwardness of speaking alone with Lord Inglewhite the day after rejecting him. He must wonder what on earth she had to say! She cleared her throat, trying to clear away her embarrassment as well. "I thought you should know that Lord Crowthorne left a parcel for me." She unwrapped the ring and held it out so that Lord Inglewhite could see.

He stepped closer to take a look, but did not touch the ring. "Ah." Something about his expression suggested he was not surprised.

"Did you know that already?" She narrowed her eyes suspiciously.

"He left a letter for me," Lord Inglewhite explained. "He confessed to being the thief, but said all the stolen objects had been restored to their proper owners. So, yes, I suspected he might have given back the ring."

Ivy handed his lordship the note Lord Crowthorne had left for her. Then she cleared her throat again. "Do you know," she asked hesitantly, "if what he writes here is true? Is he my cousin? My natural cousin, I mean?"

Lord Inglewhite studied the note for a moment before answering. Then he looked up, met her gaze, and nodded. "I believe your father must have been Alistair Bracknell, the fourth Marquis of Reading. He died in a hunting accident before you were born."

"Oh." Ivy fell silent as she absorbed that revelation. *She* was the daughter of a marquis? But the natural daughter, she reminded herself. She was only a by-blow. It was not as if the family were likely to recognize her.

Richard handed the note back to her and took the ring from her hand. He turned it about, studying the coat of arms. "According to Lord Crowthorne, Alistair told his family he intended to marry someone, but did not say whom. I suppose we will never know for certain, but he may actually have intended to marry your mother, since he had seduced her. Perhaps he really did leave her this ring as his pledge that he would return. But it seems he died before he could meet her again."

Ivy closed her eyes as she worked through all of this information. Her hands felt cold and her legs felt shaky. All her life she had believed that the unknown stranger who fathered her had intentionally abandoned her mother. What if that were not the case? What if her father were not the villain she had always thought him?

"Miss Burnley, are you quite well?"

"I think I need to sit down." Even her voice sounded tremulous.

Lord Inglewhite offered her the support of his arm, and led her to the elegant rococo sofa. She sat down and clasped her hands together, hoping to still their trembling. "I suppose it does not really change anything," she said at last. "I will never meet my father, because he is dead." A tiny hope that had long flickered in her heart died forever as she acknowledged that she would never have a chance to know her father. She had not realized until now how much she had secretly longed for that.

"No, you cannot meet *him*." Lord Inglewhite's gentle voice was both comforting and reassuring. "But doesn't it change some things? You have living relatives on your father's side. An uncle, for example. The current marquis is your father's younger brother. You might be able to meet him, if you wanted. And you have already met two of your cousins."

That was right. If Lord Crowthorne was her cousin, so was his younger brother, the vicar. A smile blossomed on Ivy's face as she speculated that Lord Francis might eventually be related to her through marriage as well as blood. He had not yet proposed to Rose, but a proposal certainly seemed imminent. That would make them cousins twice over, wouldn't it?

"Still," she murmured, speaking half to herself, "Knowing who my father was does not change who *I* am." She stared down at the familiar signet ring, which had taken on an entirely new meaning.

"No," Lord Inglewhite agreed. "It does not change your humility, your helpfulness, or your sense of honesty. You would be the same honorable, knowledgeable, and elegant young lady if your father turned out to be a dustman."

Ivy stared at him, eyes wide. "Is that how you see me?" she whispered.

He caught and held her gaze. "Yes." His tense face relaxed a trifle as he crinkled his eyes. "Why do you think I wanted to marry you?"

She opened her mouth to answer him, but could not for the life of her figure out what to say. So she shut her jaw with a snap and sat there, her heart pounding. Maybe it made no difference to Lord Inglewhite whether her father was a nobleman or a dustman, but to the rest of society, it would matter. At least a little. She would always be illegitimate, but at least she need not be ashamed of her father's social standing.

Should that matter to Ivy? Would she have responded to Lord Inglewhite's offer differently if she had known? "I suppose it shouldn't change my answer," she murmured to herself.

"Miss Burnley?" Lord Inglewhite wrinkled his face in confusion. "What do you mean?"

She looked away from him, feeling suddenly shy. She ought not have said that out loud. Time to think of a change of subject with which to distract him! She cast her eyes about the room, looking for something innocuous to ask about.

Before she thought of something to say, he pressed the issue. "Miss Burnley, when you say, 'your answer,' do you mean your response to my proposal of marriage?"

Heat rushed into her face. "Maybe," she mumbled. "I mean, yes. But of course, you said yourself that it makes no difference."

Lord Inglewhite took hold of her hand. She looked down, surprised, seeing her bare skin touching his. She would have expected sparks, shivers, or lightning bolts of sensation. Some kind of attraction undeniably connected her to Lord Inglewhite. She had felt it when they waltzed, and again when they kissed under the mistletoe on Christmas. It had struck her even this morning, every time their eyes met.

This time, though, she felt something entirely different. Rather than blazing passion, the gentle touch of Lord Inglewhite's hand felt like the comfort of a strong cup of tea, the softness of a down-filled mattress, and the heat of a warming pan at the foot of a bed, all rolled into one. The heat between them was not fervid or wild, but homely.

We could make a home together. Tears sprang to Ivy's eyes as she realized just how easy it would be to build a life with Lord Inglewhite. A good life, too: one full of domestic comfort, service to others, and both new family rituals and old traditions. She had seen enough of Lord Inglewhite in his daily life to know that they held those values in common.

"Miss Burnley."

His voice drew her attention away from that vision of happiness, back to the here and now. The furrow in his brow showed his concern, but she thought she saw something more than mere concern in his eyes.

"Yes, my lord?"

"I meant what I said earlier. It would not make a difference to me whether your father was a dustman or a duke. So far as *I* am concerned, your being the daughter of a marquis does not make you more marriageable. But I wonder—does it make a difference to *you?*"

Ivy finally recognized the light in his stained glass blue eyes. It was hope. Lord Inglewhite hoped that she had changed her mind. Ivy drew in a deep breath, feeling torn between what she wanted and what she thought was right.

"I wish I could accept you, my lord," she admitted. "I am greatly honored to have been chosen by you. I hope you realize that I am only trying to protect you. I do not think it would be wise of you to marry a woman with so great a scandal in her past." She closed her eyes, not wanting to see the look of disappointment on his face.

"What if I do not want to be wise?"

The words so surprised her that she opened her eyes. Once again, his clear blue eyes caught and held her own. She gulped nervously, but could not look away. She was not even sure that she wanted to look away.

"In that case, you must be the best judge of your own happiness." She had run out of objections and arguments. Now it was up to him. Perhaps this was what he meant on New Year's Eve, when he said that she ought to leave it to her suitor to decide whether her illegitimacy comprised an insurmountable barrier.

"What if my judgment tells me to keep you by my side forever?" He leaned forward slightly, as if to better hear her response.

The hushed intensity of Lord Inglewhite's voice made Ivy's heart hammer in her chest. But it did not scare her. On the contrary, the sound of his voice made her want to lean closer. That was her answer, wasn't it? In her heart of hearts, Ivy did not want to be wise, rational, or thoughtful about her decision. She just wanted to love and be loved.

"What then?" he prompted.

"Then . . . I suppose there is no place I would rather be than by your side," she admitted. Half terrified by the weight of the moment, half ecstatic over the happiness that lay so near at hand, she could not form any further words. Instead, she leaned forward to rest her head against his shoulder.

Lord Inglewhite cautiously wrapped one arm around her and drew her closer. She buried her face against his topcoat and took a deep breath. He smelled like cinnamon and oranges, and his embrace felt like home.

Chapter Seventeen

RICHARD HARDLY DARED to breathe. He brushed his mouth gently against Miss Burnley's glorious auburn hair, catching the scent of sweet violets. She trembled in his arms like a frightened dove, but made no motion to leave. He could have sat in silence with her for hours, except that he needed to make certain of something.

"Will you marry me, then? So that I need not ever let you go?" His voice cracked not from fear or sorrow, but from longing. He could not remember ever wanting anything more than he wanted to keep this lovely woman in his arms.

She spoke her answer so softly that he *felt* her words rather than hearing them. "Yes. I will marry you."

He closed his eyes, tightened his embrace, and said a silent prayer of gratitude. Then he blurted out the first thing that came to mind. "I suppose it is a happy Christmas after all!"

Miss Burnley giggled. "You are right. Quite the happiest Christmas I can remember." She shifted position and tipped her head back to look Richard in the eyes.

Richard could not resist lowering his head to brush a kiss against her lips. Somehow, it felt entirely different from their first kiss under the mistletoe. On his part, that Christmas Day kiss had been a declaration of interest—a warning shot fired across the bows, as it were. This kiss felt more like a direct hit: a shot to the heart.

The kiss must have affected his new fiancée similarly, because she gasped softly. When her lips parted, he caught her lower lip so he could gently deepen the kiss. Then Richard found himself enmeshed in a tangle of lips and limbs. Ivy wrapped one arm around his neck as she kissed his jawline and his chin before he caught her mouth with his again. Then he cradled her head in his hand as he kept kissing her, feeling he could not get enough. All his being was awake and clambering for more. Until this moment, he had not realized how passionately he desired her.

Very much to his disappointment, she broke the kiss by pulling away from him. He released her at once, though he would rather have kept her in his arms. They had, he supposed, gotten a little carried away in their embrace.

Her face had flushed a rosy shade, and her eyes shone brightly. "I ought to tell my aunt and uncle," she suggested. "By now they will be wondering where I am and what I have been doing."

Richard grinned, feeling uncharacteristically wicked. "I think they will guess what we have been doing. Your coiffure is a little worse for the wear." And, though it might have been his imagination, he thought her lips were a little swollen from the force of their kissing.

Yes, they had definitely gotten carried away, though he had not kissed her half as much as he wanted. Maybe he could convince her to accept a short engagement? His smile deepened as he imagined taking his new wife with him when he went to London for the Season.

Miss Burnley—no, *Ivy*—cocked her head to one side. "What are you thinking about?"

He cleared his throat. "Er, just pondering when and where we ought to get married."

She lowered her eyes charmingly, the very picture of a bashful bride. "We can think about that later, surely. It is the bride who names the date, you know."

"I know." He took hold of her hands and squeezed them

lightly. "I do not want to rush you. But I must be in London by the end of January, you know, to take my seat in Parliament."

"Oh, I had not thought of that." She frowned. "I must see what my aunt and uncle would prefer."

"Let us go down and talk to them now." Ivy was right that other guests might be speculating about their continued absence. It might be best to end their speculation. So, hand in hand, they went down to the breakfast room to announce their engagement. Now Richard could whole-heartedly look forward to tomorrow's Twelfth Night Ball. He finally had something to celebrate.

OVERNIGHT, THE GATHERING at Selwyn Castle had become an engagement ball, it being the perfect event at which to announce his betrothal to Miss Burnley. To Ivy. Just thinking about her put a foolish grin on his face.

It was a good thing Richard had such a pleasant thought to sustain him, because the rest of the day was an exhausting one. The stress began with the letter from Crowthorne that revealed him as the thief. After Richard's conversation with Crowthorne last night, this did not surprise him. Even before he read Crowthorne's confession, he had suspected that a member of the Bracknell family had stolen the jewelry. That explained why the signet ring had not been returned with the other jewels.

Unfortunately, Crowthorne's letter did not explain why he had stolen the jewels. He wrote that he needed the money for expenses his allowance did not meet, but he did not say what those expenses were. Richard could only assume that the young heir had expensive vices of some sort—gambling debts, perhaps, or a demanding mistress.

Still, the letter and Crowthorne's flight from the castle necessitated a long conversation with Squire Anderson about the next legal steps. Crowthorne was technically a commoner, his title being only a courtesy title, so he could be tried in the normal court of law. But neither Richard nor Squire Anderson were certain it would be wise to prosecute him, since all the jewels had been retrieved. None of the families involved would want the scandal made public, would they? But that might well be a moot point, depending on whether Crowthorne could be caught.

Naturally, many of the guests had questions about Crowthorne's disappearance. Richard found himself lying far more that day than he had ever done in his life. Over and over again, he assured guests that Crowthorne had been called away to the bedside of a dying friend. He had no idea whether the other houseguests accepted this Banbury tale, but he did not particularly care. If Crowthorne had wanted his flight to be thoroughly hushed up, he should have supplied a plausible reason for his absence.

In the afternoon, Richard set aside the mystery of Crowthorne's actions in order to concentrate on preparing for the ball. Rowland helped oversee the preparations for the ball, as he had promised to do. But Rowland seemed to be out of humor. He did not enliven the work with any of his usual witticisms, he answered most questions monosyllabically, and he smiled far less than was his wont.

"Is something wrong?" Richard finally asked him. "You are not yourself today."

Rowland shrugged. "We can speak of that later. For now, let us work on making this a ball to remember." But his smile did not reach his eyes. Richard could not help fretting about him.

At least the weather cooperated. The morning had been overcast but the cloud cover broke up in the afternoon. By evening, the crescent moon shone brightly in the sky. It was a pity the moon was not full; the lack of light might keep some of Richard's neighbors at home. Hopefully, a few would be bold enough to venture out despite the cold and the darkness.

As it happened, the turnout far exceeded his expectations. He had known the Andersons would be there, and the Caldwells, but he was pleasantly surprised to see people who had traveled from miles away. Naturally, he had to greet everyone in the receiving line. This involved a good deal of standing and smiling and shaking hands, all of which he found tiring.

But at least he had Ivy by his side to greet the guests. This year he introduced her to everyone as his fiancée. Next year, she would host the ball as the new countess—a prospect so pleasant, it enabled Richard to tolerate the tedium of greeting one party member after another.

Etiquette stipulated that Richard could only dance twice with Ivy, even though they were betrothed. He claimed her hand for the opening dance and for the first waltz. Then he had to watch as other gentlemen danced with her. She did not sit out a single dance. Nor did her cousin. Miss Rufford seemed to be in her element: smiling, laughing, and generally making a favorite of herself. Not surprisingly, she attracted a swarm of young men about her between sets.

Lord Francis scowled fiercely at these admirers—though perhaps his scowl had more to do with his brother's disappearance. Had Crowthorne left any kind of message for his own family? Or were the Bracknells completely in the dark as to his disappearance? Either way, his flight must have been a real blow to the family. Given the marquis's ill-health, Crowthorne might have been expected to manage the family estates.

Richard reminded himself that the Bracknell family affairs were none of his business, even if he was, in a sense, marrying into the family. He had inadvertently solved the mystery of the missing jewels, and his interest in Lord Crowthorne's affairs ended there.

The ball ended far earlier than it would have if they had been keeping Town hours instead of country hours. Even so, it was quite late by the time Richard bade farewell to the last of the guests. Under the watchful eyes of Lady Rufford, he could only give Ivy a peck on the cheek as a good-night kiss. But hopefully they would be wedded by the end of the month, and then there would be no need to part for the night at all. Richard could not remember the last time he had so happily anticipated something.

Rowland came up and slapped Richard on the back. "I think it was a smashing success. Don't you?"

"Yes, I suppose it was." Richard looked about the empty ballroom. Tomorrow, the servants would clean up the room. Tonight, though, everyone had a chance to rest. "You know, I thought this house party would be a failure," Richard admitted. "But it could have been worse, couldn't it?"

"It most certainly could have," Rowland agreed. "My team might have lost at charades!" He cocked his head to one side as he considered the possibility. "Not that that was the least bit likely."

"Oh, be quiet," Richard grumbled. "I will beat you next year. See if I don't."

To his surprise, Rowland's smile fell, and he lowered his eyes. "About that," he began.

"Yes?" Richard held his breath. Was he finally going to learn what had been bothering his brother all day?

Rowland shrugged and kept staring down at the floor. "I have been thinking it might be time for me to make a change."

"A change," Richard repeated. "You mean giving up late nights gambling at White's?" He certainly agreed Rowland ought to behave more responsibly. The excesses that might be forgiven in a boy fresh from the university did not befit a man of thirty years.

"That too." Rowland's smile was perfunctory, but at least he met Richard's eyes now. "But I meant something more significant. You know I have not made much progress in my career, Richard."

"Yes, I know." Rowland had been called to the bar several years ago, but he had tried only a few cases. Advancing as a barrister required hard work and continued study. Rowland excelled at many things, but he had never put his full heart into this profession.

"I have for some time had in mind a change of careers," Rowland continued. "And I recently heard of a business opportunity in America. One of my old university friends owns a printing press in Boston, and he is looking for a partner." This time, Rowland's smile looked genuine. "You know I have always had a literary bent."

Richard nodded. It could not be denied that Rowland had both a gift for writing comic verse and a turn for satirical description. Even before he learned that Rowland had taken to writing book reviews, Richard had suspected that some of the wittiest of the anonymous letters to the editor of *The Times* were written by his brother.

"Anyway," Rowland continued, "I thought I might as well give the literary profession a try, since I never took to the law the way Father hoped."

"But Boston?" Richard protested. "You are thinking of going to *America?* How long would you stay?"

Rowland shrugged. "Depends on how well the work suits me, I suppose. I might stay only a few months. Or I might stay forever."

"Forever." Richard knew he sounded like a parrot, but he could not think of anything else to say. He had already lost one brother to a tragic death. He did not want to lose his remaining brother to emigration. "But why America?"

Rowland would not meet his eyes. He looked down and scuffed the floor with the tip of his dancing slipper. "As I said, I think a change would be good for me."

He was concealing something. Richard was certain of it. But what could possibly drive Rowland to leave the country so suddenly? When he finally made the connection, Richard drew in a sharp breath.

"You are following Crowthorne." It came out as a statement, not a question.

"I can neither confirm nor deny that." Rowland shrugged his shoulders again and continued to evade Richard's gaze.

That was all the confirmation that Richard needed. "I see."

He did see a good deal now. Such as why Rowland had so often chosen to walk or sit by Lord Crowthorne's side during the house party. Such as what secret Crowthorne might have been so bitter about. Could this revelation even explain the jewel thefts?

"Was someone blackmailing Lord Crowthorne?" Richard asked. "Making him pay to keep his . . . proclivities. . . secret?" It was a nasty thought, but it seemed entirely possible. There were, unfortunately, many nasty people in the world.

Blackmail would explain Crowthorne's need for funds in excess of his allowance. Sexual relations between men were illegal and punishable by death. If the wrong person knew about Crowthorne's inclinations, the young heir might pay very dearly to keep the secret. Assuming, of course, Richard's guesses were accurate. He really had no evidence to support his assumption, except for Rowland's changing facial expressions. But he did not think he misread the situation.

Rowland grimaced and kept looking away. "I can neither confirm nor deny that, either."

Richard interpreted that as a "yes." It made a good deal of sense. Perhaps in America, Crowthorne would feel safe from his blackmailer. Richard hoped that would really be the case. Crowthorne deserved to live his life free of persecution. But why must Rowland go running after him?

Richard sighed, accepting that Rowland must be the best judge of his own happiness. "I will miss you very much if you go." Perhaps, though, America would be good for Rowland. Certainly, the legal profession had not worked out well for him.

Rowland finally looked up and met his gaze. "I will miss you, too. And miss getting to see my nieces and nephews when they are born." Richard glanced away in embarrassment, and Rowland's tense smile relaxed into something far more like his usual mischievous grin. "But I promise I will stay in England for your wedding. I wouldn't miss that for the world!"

Chapter Eighteen

January 29, 1816

ON THE LAST Monday in January, Ivy's friends, relatives, and neighbors crowded the sanctuary of St. Sebastian's parish to watch her marry the Earl of Inglewhite. Elderly Mr. King, who had been the vicar all of Ivy's life, presided over the ceremony. Mr. Hawkins played the organ, as he had since time immemorial, and some of Ivy's own Sunday School students were hired to ring a wedding peal when the ceremony ended.

It might have been the most bittersweet moment of Ivy's life. She truly had not expected to have to leave her childhood home behind so soon, if at all. For years, she'd assumed her place in life lay with her uncle and aunt, as the dutiful niece who would look after them as they aged. She had expected to stay at Rufford Manor long after Rose married and left for a home of her own.

Instead, she stood before the altar with the sweetest, tenderest, handsomest man she had ever met, listening as he promised to love her, comfort her, honor her, and keep her all their lives. She could not believe her good fortune. Indeed, she half feared that some cruel twist of fate would occur at the eleventh hour to prevent their marriage. But no such thing transpired.

On the contrary, all the fates cooperated to keep the roads

dry for travel and all the important members of the wedding hale and good tempered. Though January was a gloomy month for a wedding, this day felt glorious. The sun sent a few stray sunbeams through the stained glass window over the altar, gently illuminating the bridal couple.

Ivy spent much of the ceremony blinking away the tears that threatened to trickle out of her eyes. Even she could not have said whether she wept for the grief of leaving the only home she'd ever known or for the joy of marrying a man who had already grown so dear to her. They would have the rest of their lives to learn to love each other more and more.

She cried even harder at the end of the wedding breakfast, when she bade farewell to her aunt, uncle, and cousins. *Both* her cousins, since Lord Francis attended the wedding as Miss Rufford's intended. He had proposed the day after the Twelfth Night ball, claiming to have been inspired by Richard and Ivy's example of betrothed bliss. He and Rose planned to marry after Easter, giving Lord Francis time to prepare the vicarage for his new bride. Knowing that Rose would live within walking distance of Selwyn Castle felt like the final blessed drop that made the cup of Ivy's joy overflow.

As if that were not enough weeping, Ivy burst into tears *again* when Rufford Manor disappeared around a bend in the road as their traveling chariot took them towards London and their new life together. She would probably visit the manor occasionally in the future, but it would never again be her home. For someone strongly attached to both place and tradition, that was a genuine loss.

Richard pulled a handkerchief out of his pocket and wiped her tears away. Then he kissed her tear-stained face. The sweet warmth of his touch put an end to Ivy's pain, and she ceased crying.

"My dear, is becoming my wife really cause for so many tears?" His gentle smile showed that he spoke in jest.

"You know perfectly well I am not crying because I have

become your wife!" she protested. "I am delighted to be married to you—"

He interrupted her with a kiss on the lips. She licked his lower lip in response, and suddenly their embrace went from comforting to arousing. They became increasingly distracted and Ivy did not get to finish her explanation until they broke apart to catch their breath.

Ivy tried to repair her ravaged coiffure, but she soon gave it up as a lost cause. "It is just hard to move to a new home when one has lived in the same place all one's life," she explained. A frown tugged at the corners of her mouth. "I suppose I will never have another Christmas at Rufford Manor."

Richard smiled as he gently pushed a loose strand of her hair away from her eyes. "Perhaps not, but, Lord willing, you will have many more Christmases at Selwyn Castle."

And that, Ivy agreed, was a prospect worth looking forward to.

The End

About the Author

Anne Rollins is the pen name of an English professor who lives in Northern California with her family, too many cats, and an enormous collection of books. She has spent untold hours of her life rereading Georgette Heyer novels, and hopes that someday people will compulsively reread her novels, too!

Join me at the following:
annerollins.com
facebook.com/profile.php?id=100094523334798
instagram.com/annerollins23
threads.net/@annerollins23